the scent of magic

D1040640

Also by Cliff McNish

The Doomspell

The Wizard's Promise
(September 2002)

the scent of magic

Cliff McNish

Dolphin

First published in Great Britain in 2001
by Orion Children's Books
This paperback edition first published 2002 by Dolphin Paperbacks
a division of the Orion Publishing Group Ltd
Orion House
5 Upper St Martin's Lane
London WC2H 9EA

A catalogue record for this book is available
from the British Library

Printed in Great Britain by
Clays Ltd, St Ives plc

ISBN 1 84255 054 3

For Ciara, for everything

contents

1 Eyes 1

2 Ool 13

3 Magic without Rules 26

4 The Camberwell Beauty 41

5 Fish without Armour 45

6 The Hairy Fly 53

7 The Blue-Sky Rainbow 64

8 The Stone Angel 73

9 Games without Limits 82

10 The Finest Child 100

11 Ambush 113

12 Ocean 128

13 Battle 139

14 Victim 151

15 Arrivals 163

16 Imprisonment 169

17 The Trap 175

18 The Butterfly Child 187

19 Awakening 197

20 Flight 204

1

eyes

'Rachel, wake up, get out of the dream!' Morpeth shook her gently, then more roughly when she did not move. 'Come on, wake up!'

'What?' Rachel's eyes half-opened.

Briefly Morpeth saw the remains of her nightmare. It dug into her cheek, as big as a dog: the gnarled black claw of a Witch. As Morpeth watched the thick green fingernails faded on Rachel's pale face.

'It's all right,' he said hastily, gripping her shoulders. 'Don't be afraid. You're safe, at home, in your room. There's no Witch.'

Rachel jerked awake and sat up, her breath coming in hurried gasps.

'Oh, Morpeth,' she murmured, '*never* wake me up like that. When I'm dreaming...I might...I could have hurt you.' She buried her face in a pillow, waiting until the cold jagged sensation of the fingernails had gone. 'You should know better,' she said at last. 'A spell might have slipped out.'

'Would you rather your mum faced those claws?' he answered. 'At least I can recognize them.'

Rachel nodded bleakly. 'But it's dangerous, even for you. Always let me wake up naturally, when I'm ready.'

Morpeth grunted, pointing at the sunlight filtering through the curtains. 'I waited as long as I could. Half the day's gone, and your mum was just about to get you up.' He picked a few strands of weed from her hair. 'Interesting smell these have.'

'Oh no,' groaned Rachel, noticing the staleness for the first time. 'I was in the pond again last night, wasn't I?'

'I'm afraid so.'

Rachel bit her lip. 'That's twice this week.'

'Three times.'

'I suppose I had the gills?'

'Yes, the usual scarlet ones, on your neck.'

'Ugh!' Rachel felt below her ears in disgust. 'How long was I under the water this time?'

'About an hour.'

'An *hour*!' Rachel shook her head grimly. 'Then it's getting worse. All right, I'm up.' She listened for a second. 'Will you check the corridor and bathroom are clear?'

Morpeth nipped out, returning moments later. 'Nobody about, and here's a couple of fresh towels. I'll stuff last night's sheets in the wash, shall I?'

Rachel smiled, taking the towels. 'Morpeth, you're my guardian angel.'

Slipping quietly into the bathroom, she used a long hot shower to remove the stink of the pond. Returning to her room, she sat beside the dressing-table mirror, half-heartedly brushing out her long straight dark hair.

Then she stopped. She put the brush down. She turned slowly to the mirror and examined her slim, lightly freckled face.

The eyes that gazed back were no longer quite human. Her old hazel-green eyes, matching her dad's, had gone. Replacing them were her new magical eyes. Spells clustered in the corners, behind the lids. They liked it there, where they could look out onto the world. Throughout the day they crowded forward, eager for her attention. Each spell had its own unique colour. Yesterday's spell-colours had started off scarlet and gold, surrounding her black pupil. This morning there was no pupil at all. There was only a deep wide blue in both eyes, the shade of a summer sky. Rachel had seen that colour many times recently. It was the colour of a flying spell, aching to be used.

Staring at her reflection in the mirror, Rachel said, 'No. I won't fly. I made a promise, I'm keeping it. I won't give in to you!'

'Give in to who?' asked a voice.

Rachel turned, startled. Her mum stood behind her, staring anxiously into the mirror.

'Mum, where did you come from?'

'I've been here awhile, just watching you. And *them*.' Mum studied Rachel's spell-drenched eyes. Their colour had now changed to a mournful grey. 'Those spells,' Mum said angrily. 'What are they expecting from you? Why won't they just leave you in peace for once?'

'It's all right, Mum,' Rachel mumbled vaguely. 'I'm … I'm still in charge of them.'

Mum wrapped her arms around Rachel's neck. Holding her tight, she said in the softest of voices, 'Then tell me why you're trembling? Do you think after twelve years I can't tell when my own daughter's hurting?'

A single tear rolled down Rachel's cheek. She tried to dash the wetness away.

'Let it out,' Mum said. 'You cry it out. Those terrible spells. How dare they do anything to harm you!'

For a few minutes Rachel leaned back into her mother's embrace. Finally she said, 'I'm all right, really I am. I'm fine. I am.'

Mum squeezed Rachel again and simply stood there, obviously reluctant to leave.

'You won't keep staring in that mirror?'

'No more staring today,' Rachel answered, forcing a smile. 'Promise.' As Mum walked slowly to the door, she said, 'You're missing Dad, aren't you?'

Mum halted at the door. 'Is it that obvious?'

'Only because I miss him too. I hate it when he's away.'

'His last foreign contract this year's nearly finished,' Mum told her. 'He'll be back in a month or so.'

'Thirty-eight days,' Rachel said.

Mum smiled conspiratorially. 'So we both count!' She turned to leave. 'Hurry down, will you? I've had just about enough of Eric and the prapsies today. I do love your brother, but he's nine going on six half the time, the things he teaches those child-birds.' She tramped back downstairs, muttering all the way.

4

Rachel finished dressing and made her way to the kitchen. As soon as she entered the prapsies covered their faces.

'Lock away your sparky eyes!' one shrieked, glimpsing her.

Oops, Rachel thought, quickly switching the glowing spell-colours off.

The other prapsy flapped irritably in front of her face. 'Eric could have been blinded!' it squeaked. 'His handsome face could have eye-holes burned in it!'

Rachel knew better than to react in any way. She put some bread on the grill and watched it brown, as if toasting bread fascinated her.

The prapsies hovered next to her nose, pulling faces. They were odd, mixed-up things, the joke creation of a Witch who had once used them as messengers. Bodily they were identical to crows, with the typical sleek, blue-black feathers. But instead of beaks they had noses; and instead of bird-faces, theirs were plump, dimpled and rosy-cheeked, with soft lips. Each prapsy had the head of a baby.

Mum swished by, waving the child-birds out of her way. They parted, then came back together, hovering perfectly over Rachel's head. One blew a raspberry; the other accidentally dribbled on her toast.

'How delightful,' Rachel said, throwing the slice in the bin. 'I wish I knew how they grew their baby-faces back again. I preferred it when they just squawked.'

Both prapsies showed her their toothless gums.

'Gaze at us, chimp face!' they cooed. 'We're so gorgeous. We're so beautiful! Ask Eric.'

Eric sat nearby at the kitchen table, casually turning the pages of a comic.

'You all right, sis?' he asked, glancing up. 'Enjoying the boys' company?'

'I'm fine,' she said dryly. 'But I'd prefer not to be within kissing distance. Do you think you might call the boys off long enough for me to butter my toast?'

'Sure thing.' He whistled.

Instantly both prapsies flew onto his shoulders. They perched there, scowling at Rachel.

'And shut them up for ten minutes,' Mum said in her deadliest voice. 'Or it's crow stew tonight.'

Eric pretended not to hear, but he did finger-zip his mouth. The prapsies sucked their lips in tight to prevent any more insults escaping.

Eric was a short stocky boy with a tough expression he often practised. His most striking feature was his hair – a blond mass of curls. Eric hated his hair. Mothers liked to touch the soft waviness of it. In a couple of years he was determined to get the locks hacked off. A skinhead. For now he had to be content with the prapsies messing it up as often as possible with their claws.

'I suppose the prapsies *slept* with you again last night?' Rachel said witheringly.

'Of course.' Eric grinned – and so did the prapsies – imitating him with eerie precision.

'I've watched them,' Rachel went on. 'They sit on your bed, with those big baby eyes. It's spooky. They copy everything you do. When you turn, they turn. They even imitate your snoring.'

'Ah, it's true,' Eric chuckled, 'They adore me.' He clicked his fingers. One prapsy immediately nudged the page of his comic over with its small upturned nose.

'Pathetic,' Rachel muttered. 'Three morons. Where's Morpeth?'

'I could tell you,' Eric replied. 'But what's in it for me?'

'He's in the garden,' Mum said, clipping Eric round the ear. She handed Rachel some freshly buttered toast. 'Eat a crust before you go out, won't you?'

After breakfast Rachel wandered into the back garden. It was a bakingly hot July day, with almost all of the summer holidays still left. Morpeth lay spread out by the pond. He was a thin boy, with startlingly blue eyes and thick sandy hair sticking out in all directions. An ice-cool drink lay within easy reach of his bronze arm.

Rachel smiled affectionately. 'I see you've settled in for the summer.'

'Thanks to Dragwena, I missed out on several hundred summers,' Morpeth said. 'I'm catching up as best I can.' He pulled a can of coke out of the pond and handed it to Rachel. 'I've been saving this. How are you feeling?'

'Pretty grim,' she said, easing into the garden hammock.

'You certainly smell better. I suppose you scrubbed with soap?'

'Yes, Morpeth, I did,' Rachel said, laughing. 'Why? Don't you?'

'Still can't stand the slimy feel,' he admitted. 'That funny sweet smell too, there's something wrong about it. Of course, we didn't have soap when I was a boy. Everyone smelt awful and no one cared a bit.'

Rachel couldn't quite get used to this new child-Morpeth. She had met him a year before on another world: Ithrea. Rachel shuddered even now to think of that desolate world of dark snow. A hated Witch, Dragwena, had ruled there. Morpeth had been her reluctant servant.

For centuries he had been forced to watch as Dragwena abducted children from our world. Rachel and Eric were the last to be kidnapped. When she arrived, Rachel discovered that all children possess magic they cannot use on Earth. That was why the Witch wanted them – to serve her own purposes. Morpeth had tutored Rachel, and she blossomed, discovering that she was more magically gifted than any child who had come before – the first strong enough to truly resist Dragwena. Eric, too, had a gift, and this time it was one no other child possessed. Uniquely, he could unmake spells. He could *destroy* them. In a final terrifying battle Rachel and Eric had fought the Witch's Doomspell and witnessed the death of Dragwena at the hands of the great Wizard, Larpskendya.

As Rachel gazed at Morpeth now, it was difficult for her to remember that for hundreds of years he had been a wrinkled old man kept alive only by the Witch's magic. Somehow he had defied the worst of Dragwena's influence, and when Rachel and Eric arrived he risked his life over and over for them. In gratitude, the Wizard Larpskendya gave Morpeth back all the lost years of childhood Dragwena had taken from him. He returned, as a boy, home – but not his own home. His original family were long dead, of course. So Rachel's parents had secretly adopted him – and here he was, a year later, a man-boy in a summer garden. A few other creatures had chosen to return from Ithrea with Rachel and Eric. Only the prapsies remained. The wolf-cub, Scorpa, Ronnocoden the eagle, and a few worms, had soon disappeared, deciding to make a new life amongst their own kind on Earth.

'What's wrong?' Rachel asked, noticing that Morpeth looked slightly uncomfortable.

'It's these shorts,' he pouted. 'Your mum forgets that I'm five-hundred-and-thirty-seven years old. I don't *like* stripy pants.'

'You couldn't wear your old leathers from Ithrea forever, Morpeth. You've outgrown them.'

'But they *felt* good,' he said. 'These shorts just look stupid. They don't fit properly, either. Your mum always assumes I'm the same size as Eric.'

'Are they too tight?'

'Too loose,' Morpeth said meaningfully.

'Mm. Dangerous.' Rachel smiled. 'Must tell Mum about that … of course, you could go to the shops and buy your own.'

Morpeth gave her a grouchy shrug. Shopping meant setting foot out of the house and across the dreaded street. Traffic unnerved him. There had been no cars when he was a boy, or aeroplanes. The sheer *noisiness* of modern life made him constantly edgy, and he avoided roads whenever possible.

For a few minutes Rachel lay in the hammock next to the pond, simply enjoying the sunshine and the light breeze blowing over her legs.

'Morpeth,' she said at last, 'I was in bed for fifteen hours last night. I can't wake up. These things my spells are doing while I'm asleep ... what's happening?'

'You know the answer to that,' he said bluntly.

Rachel shook her head. 'I know my spells want to be used,' she said. 'But they've behaved until now. What's changed? Why are they suddenly taking over like this?'

'They're defying you,' he answered. 'They're restless, impatient. Magic isn't something you can just tame like a pet, Rachel. Especially *your* magic.' He leant across and tapped her head. 'Your spells are far too intense, too ambitious, to leave you alone for long. And you stopped listening to their requests months ago, didn't you? You locked them out completely.'

'I had to,' Rachel protested. 'They were too tempting. Larpskendya made me promise not to use my spells—'

'I know,' Morpeth said. 'But your spells don't care about a promise made to a Wizard. They don't like being ignored. You won't listen while you're awake, so they come out to play at night – when they can take charge of your dreams.'

Rachel bent across to stir the surface of the pond. 'But why dump me under water?'

'Why not?' Morpeth said. 'Water must be an interesting place for bored spells to experiment. There's the challenge of how to enable you to breathe without lungs. And how to enable you to inhale water without damaging your body. Those things are difficult. They require many intricate spells, co-operating closely.'

Rachel thought of the gills. 'I can handle them,' she

insisted. 'Larpskendya warned me a party of Witches could detect my spells, even from space. That might lead the Witches to all children. I won't break my promise!'

'You already *have*,' snorted Morpeth. He stood up. 'You must take back control, Rachel. Give your spells something to do – room to breathe at least. And do it while you're awake, and you can restrain them.'

'Nothing terrible's happened yet…'

Morpeth met her gaze. 'Are you going to wait until it does? I know you wouldn't strike out deliberately, Rachel, but what about your nightmares? What if your mum tried to wake you at the wrong time? This morning, for instance. Anything could have occurred. I saw the claw.' He stared earnestly at her. 'That's your worst nightmare, isn't it? And mine too: in my darkest dreams I'm facing Dragwena again. I'm hunted by a Witch.'

Rachel shivered. She tried never to think of Dragwena.

Bringing the drink of Coke to her lips, she noticed a wasp. It buzzed around the lid of the can, crawled under the tab and finally fell into the drink. Rachel sighed, absently tipping the wasp onto the grass.

'What spells just came into your head?' Morpeth asked sharply.

'Only the usual ones.'

'Such as?'

'Four spells: one to kill the wasp; a second to rescue it; a third to disinfect the can.' She watched the wasp, wings fizzing, stagger across the lawn, and smiled. 'And a warming spell to dry the insect's wings.'

'Which spell came first to mind?'

The killing spell, thought Rachel, and Morpeth read the answer in her face.

'I wouldn't have hurt the wasp,' she told him.

'I know,' said Morpeth. 'But it's interesting that the most dangerous spells offer themselves first. They always dominate the others.'

Rachel leaned over the pond and gazed at her reflection. Her eyes had turned a deep brown, like moistened sand. She looked for more vibrant colours, but her spells were unusually reticent – as if they did not want her spying on them. Why should that be?

For the first time in months Rachel turned her attention inward. What are you up to? she demanded. Several spells became silent, tucking themselves slyly away, not wishing her to recognize the mischief they planned.

They're waiting, Rachel realized – waiting until I fall asleep.

To Morpeth, she said, 'You'd better keep a close eye on me tonight.'

2

Ool

Heebra, mother of Dragwena, gazed out of the eye-shaped window of her tower.

Beneath her, in all its vast glory, lay Ool, home of the Witches. It was a freezing world. Dark grey snow plunged from the sky, filling the air, squeezing out virtually all light. Heebra had ruled for over two thousand years, and in all that time the snow had never ceased to fall. Valleys overflowed with it; animals quaked and bred under it; the tallest mountains of Ool had long ago been swallowed under its dismal bitter flakes.

Only the towers of the Witches rose above the snows.

As Heebra gazed out of the window her younger daughter, Calen, emerged from the shadows of the chamber.

'Will we watch the students fight?' Calen asked eagerly.

'So early? They were told to prepare for a night contest.'

'Let's surprise them, Mother. Make them fight now!'

Heebra smiled indulgently and signalled for the contestants to be made ready.

While she waited, Heebra surveyed the cold magnificence of Ool. The jutting towers of her Witches thronged the sky. Each tower was topped by an emerald eye-window, its height marking the status of the Witch who lived inside. There were millions of towers, but Heebra's outreached them all. It rose thick and black from the everlasting snows, decorated by the countless faces of the Witches she had defeated in battle. In Heebra's early rule many Witches had challenged her possession of the Great Tower. None dared any longer. A pity: it had been a long time since she had the pleasure of carving a new face into the stone.

Calen joined her by the window. 'Do you remember winning your first eye, Mother? A legendary battle!'

Heebra shrugged. 'It was nothing. A small tower. A lump of rock. Just a few hundred feet, and painfully thin.'

'Who cares about the size! You defeated twelve other students to win it.' Calen looked admiringly at her mother. 'No one had ever done that before. You were incredible, even then.'

Heebra studied Calen. It made her ache to see how much like her fabulous lost daughter Dragwena she had become. At less than four hundred years of age, Calen was a High Witch in her prime. Her skin was still blood-red, having lost none of its freshness. Her vision also perfect, the tattooed eyes glowing under their bone-ridged brows. Even her sense of smell remained intact; sensitive nostrils, shaped like slashed tulip petals, could sniff out live meat hiding under the deepest snow. But perhaps Calen's best features were her jaws. All four were in spectacular condition. Despite numerous battles not one of the curved triangular black teeth had been lost or scratched. They glistened in her well-oiled silver gums, cleaned by armoured spiders that were supremely healthy, jumping alertly between the jaws in search of food scraps.

Heebra turned her attention to Nylo, Calen's soul-snake. He was restless, this one, like his mistress, a supple yellow body always on the move about her throat.

For all young Witches, Heebra knew their soul-snake was precious: as advisor, friend, shield and weapon – and a second set of watchful eyes. Most Witches needed their soul-snakes to be active throughout their lives. Heebra had long ago dispensed with Mak, her own snake. He was now golden and solid, hanging nearly lifeless against her breast. This, more than anything else, signified the magnitude of Heebra's power.

She drew her thoughts back to the eye-window.

'Well?' she asked. 'Do I know any of those in today's contest?'

'I doubt it,' said Calen. 'It's only a few students from the Advanced levels.'

Heebra smiled. 'Why do you always insist on observing such juvenile battles? Their spells are so uninteresting.'

'It's their passion I enjoy,' Calen answered. 'Don't you remember how thrilling it felt to win a blood-contest, mother?'

Heebra let her mind wander back. Once she had been

like today's students – aching for a chance to fight for her first eye. How she had relished that victory! Crushing her opponent, throwing out the dead Witch's servants, and living in *her* tower, still warm from her presence, with so many future contests and more elegant towers beckoning…

The three Advanced students were ready. Raising long bare arms, they flew to appointed starting positions in the sky, their sapphire battle dresses fluttering in the winds.

'Who do you think will win?' Calen asked, waiting for the contest to begin.

'It doesn't matter,' Heebra said. 'None are talented enough to get to the next level of magic.'

'How can you tell?'

As soon as Calen said this Heebra ripped Nylo from her neck. She stretched his jaw until it almost snapped. Calen waited fearfully, knowing that she had no spell powerful enough to threaten her mother.

With disdain, Heebra said, '*How can I tell?* I expect finer judgement than that from one who is to rule after me. You should be able to tell immediately! The mediocre quality of the students' flight alone shows that none will make a High Witch.'

Calen lowered her gaze. 'Of course. I should have recognized that.'

Heebra flung Nylo contemptuously across the chamber. Calen picked him up, though she didn't dare comfort him in front of her mother.

Together, in charged silence, they turned towards the battle.

Evening had settled in, so both switched to night-vision. Slowly their tattooed eyes stretched across their cheekbones, meeting at the back of bald pitted skulls. Heebra and Calen could now follow the contest with ease. The students began, hiding in the dense storm-whirls of the upper atmosphere, launching their spells, breathlessly attacking and defending.

Heebra did not care. Annoyed with Calen, her mind turned as it so often did to her elder daughter, Dragwena. Where was she? Dragwena had ventured alone into the realms of remote space to conquer new worlds. For centuries Heebra had waited expectantly for her return. Later she sent out search parties, but they never found her. Standing here, watching the young students above struggling to survive in the charcoal grainy sky, Heebra's chest suddenly tightened. Was her superb, wild Dragwena still alive somewhere? Or did she lie dead on some hateful world, with no snow to anoint her grave?

'Do you want me to pause the contest?' Calen asked, sensing her mother's mood.

'No,' sighed Heebra. 'Let them finish.'

'It won't be long. All three students are starting to make mistakes.'

Heebra nodded, losing interest. What was the point of sharpening and practising their magic, she thought in sudden frustration, without any *Wizards* to fight? Her Witches had been slowly losing the endless war against the Wizards for millennia. In Heebra's own lifetime the Sisterhood had lost seven worlds they had previously conquered. Seven! Each time the Wizards retreated before her fleetest warriors could catch them. If only her Witches could find Orin Fen, the Wizard home world! But the location was unknown. Larpskendya, the Wizard leader, had moved the Wizards from their original planet, and obscured the way to their new one. Gradually, almost bloodlessly, he was winning the war – pushing her best Witches back, back, closer to Ool. The grip of the Witches had never been weaker.

'A defeat,' laughed Calen. 'At last!'

One of the students, her face flushed with excitement, drifted towards Heebra's tower. In her claws she carried the lifeless soul-snakes of the other students like trophies. But her moment of triumph was spoiled.

High in the sky a tiny green ball of light wandered through the clouds. Glowing intermittently, it staggered through the air as if in distress.

Heebra and Calen immediately forgot about the victorious student and flew from the eye-tower to meet the ball.

Calen gasped. 'It can't be!'

'It is!' marvelled Heebra.

All the Witches who had been following the student contest fell silent. None had ever seen this before: a dead Witch, her life-force returning. Only twice in the ancient history of Ool had such a long journey been made from space. What living Witch could have the strength to have travelled so far?

'Dragwena!' Heebra cried.

Her heart spasming with joy, she placed the green light lovingly on one of her tongues. Still breathing, Heebra realized. Still alive.

The injured life-force trembled inside, too frail to speak.

'Be well, my daughter,' Heebra comforted. 'You are home now.'

Inside the Great Tower Heebra unrolled her tongue carefully onto the hard floor.

At once the green ball started to stretch and grow at a fantastic rate. Dragwena's thighs bulged, forced their way out, the muscles soft, trying to harden.

'How she fights!' Calen marvelled. 'Look how she wants to live!'

Finally the transformation was finished – but Dragwena was incomplete.

'She has come too far to survive,' realized Heebra. 'She's too weak!'

The upper half of Dragwena's body was only half-formed. She had a single arm. The useless claw at the end of it flapped feebly in the air. Her eyes were covered in skin that would never open. Useless lungs lay collapsed inside her body. But her brain – the thing that had driven her all this way – was already fully developed. Dragwena could think. Somehow she heaved herself to a sitting position. She raised her malformed head, trying to draw breath. When Dragwena realized she could not do so she began to jerk pitifully.

Heebra ran across the chamber and supported Dragwena's head, while Calen fired renewal spells. But Dragwena was so weak that the spells merely injured her more.

She lay in her mother's arms, waiting to die.

'How could she be in this condition?' wailed Calen. 'She must have travelled further than any Witch before. Oh, sister!'

'Yes. There must be an extraordinary reason for her to have laboured so long.' Heebra gripped Dragwena's head and made a mind-connection. 'What happened?' she demanded. 'Who did this to you?'

Dragwena fought through her panic. She formed several images: Rachel, Eric, Larpskendya and the patterns of their magic. She formed a picture of the world of Ithrea and showed her mother the bitterness of her final moments there. The images shattered as Dragwena's oxygen-starved brain started to die.

'Not yet!' screamed Heebra. 'Not yet! Where is this world? Show us!'

Dragwena clutched her mother's soul-snake, her body shaking. A dim representation formed in Heebra's mind, marking the path between alien constellations – from Ool to Ithrea, and from Ithrea on to a larger blue planet with swirling clouds and filled with children – Earth.

Then Dragwena's four jaws flopped open. Heebra held her close, nearly crushing her daughter's body with love and anger. Dragwena's mind became dark, but she managed to flash a final image. It was a picture of the Dragwena of old, at the height of her powers, standing confidently next to her mother as they gazed down together over the vast skyline of the eye-towers. The wind swept through their shimmering black dresses, and their diamond and golden soul-snakes were playfully intertwined. They were invincible.

The image faded and Dragwena died.

Heebra sat entirely motionless for several minutes. She simply held her daughter. She said nothing. She barely breathed. When she did stand up Calen, almost blind with grief herself, stood well back in the chamber, knowing the power of the frenzy coming.

And how it came! Heebra burst out of the eye-tower window, carrying her rage. Streaking across Ool's black skies she headed everywhere and nowhere, out of control, lamenting through the blizzards. No other Witches dared fly that whole night, and for the first time in over a thousand years Mak stirred himself and held her in his scaly embrace.

Calen spent the night burying her dead sister's heart.

As tradition required she cupped it in one of her mouths, and used only her claws to dig down to the deepest ice under the snow. Here even the largest burrowing animals could never reach Dragwena's body. Then Calen flew back to the Great Tower, cultivating her anguish and hatred, and wondering what mood to expect from her mother.

Shortly after daybreak Heebra returned. Her face was now entirely calm, almost expressionless. She told Calen about everything Dragwena had shown her.

'Then we can find this Rachel and Eric and revenge her death!' exulted Calen. 'Let me go. The girl-child will be easy enough to find. Her reek was all over Dragwena's body.'

Heebra raked her claws thoughtfully against Mak. 'We will enjoy that pleasure soon enough. Dragwena travelled a remarkable distance to reach us. I doubt the desire for revenge alone carried her so far. I believe she wanted to tell us about this place called Earth. Only a Wizard has ever challenged a High Witch in personal combat, yet this Rachel child-creature found a way through Dragwena's defences. Think of that! We must find out more about these intriguing children.'

'If they are talented Larpskendya will protect them well.'

'No doubt.' Heebra laughed. 'Larpskendya will protect them anyway, even if they are useless. Feeble creatures always attract his sympathy.'

'Do you think Dragwena left Ithrea unnoticed?'

'She must have done. Larpskendya would never endanger its children by permitting Dragwena to escape.'

'In that case,' said Calen, 'the Wizards will not be expecting us.'

'They will,' mused Heebra. 'Larpskendya plans for everything.' She rolled a spider meditatively on her tongue. 'However, Ithrea is the closer world. Larpskendya would expect us to arrive there first. To surprise him we will bypass Ithrea, leave it in peace for now.'

'Even so, he is bound to leave some defences on Earth itself,' Calen said.

'True. How can we draw him away from there?' Heebra's eyes shone. 'What would terrify Larpskendya most?'

Calen stared blankly.

'The Griddas,' said Heebra.

At the mention of this name Nylo contracted, becoming a tight shivering curl around Calen's neck. Gridda Witches were considered almost demonic, even by the fiercest of Ool's other Witches. They were the largest and most savage of all the Sisterhood, their orange faces and hulking brown bodies unmistakable. Bred in small numbers, they were locked underground, only ever intended to be used as a last line of defence if Ool itself was besieged – or to lead the attack on Orin Fen, if the High Witches ever discovered the Wizard home world.

Calen stroked Nylo soothingly. 'We can't release the Griddas,' she protested. 'They're unpredictable. Even a few … will create havoc.'

'Exactly,' said Heebra. 'That is the point. We will spread them wide, let them bring fear to as many worlds as they can quickly reach.'

'Mother, once their rage begins, the Griddas will be impossible to control. They may kill thousands.'

'I don't care how many they kill,' said Heebra. 'None of the other worlds have creatures like this Rachel. The point is that Larpskendya *will* care. He will be forced to use most of the Wizards to stop the Griddas. That will leave Earth vulnerable.' She stared at Nylo, then faced her daughter. 'What route should we take to Rachel's world? If you ruled, what would you advise?'

Calen looked uncertain. 'We should take our time,' she suggested. 'Move stealthily, avoiding our usual meeting places and rest sanctuaries in space. A scouting group would be best – just five or six Witches, difficult to detect. And when we arrive on this Earth world I would advise that we not kill Rachel and Eric immediately. They are too obviously targets for our revenge. Larpskendya may be watching them closely. We should start by observing the other children. Let's see what they have to offer. We can deal with Rachel and Eric, and the third, Morpeth, when we are ready.'

Heebra smiled. 'Good. Who should lead the scout group?'

Calen hesitated.

'One more surprise for Larpskendya,' said Heebra. 'I will lead it. He will never expect that. I'll lead the way to Earth myself. Go. Instruct the Sisterhood of our plans.'

Heebra knew the journey would be a long one. She selected only the most durable and fiercely loyal High Witches to accompany her. Within days the preparations to leave were complete, and the chosen Witches, fed and ready, gathered together in the howling winds and lightning of a huge storm-whirl that touched the edge of space. Impatiently they awaited the signal to depart.

First Heebra launched the Gridda Witches. She sent them out in all directions simultaneously. Led by their pack-leader, Gultrathaca, the Griddas moved out in hunting teams, shrieking joyfully, their heavily muscled bodies coiled with power.

When they had gone Heebra gestured for the scouting party to move out into the darkness of space. Seeing her best Witches together like this reminded Heebra of the glorious wars of the past. Feeling young, she led from the front and, as the group moved in a graceful line away from Ool, Heebra considered what she had learned about the child, Rachel.

From Dragwena she knew the pattern of Rachel's magic. When they arrived on Earth the girl would be easy to find. And on the journey there would be endless time to decide the most fitting way to kill her.

3

MAGIC
WITHOUT RULES

Morpeth lay fully clothed on his bed, alert and waiting. Even so he almost missed the faint sound. It was the rustle of hair moving against a ceiling.

He opened his door a crack and peered out.

Rachel floated in the corridor. The top of her scalp seemed to be anchored to the ceiling. Beneath it her body, wrapped in a pale yellow nightdress, swayed in a leisurely way. It was if her bones had become so weightless that the slightest motion of air could tilt and bend them. Her arms and legs drifted with the same relaxed rocking rhythm, like the motion of seaweed under waves.

Morpeth stepped into the corridor, careful to make no

sudden noises. Rachel's eyes were shut, but the skin of the lids jerked violently from side to side: a dream. Peering more closely, he saw her hair lift and move. Strands of it had bunched together and were rising from her head, feeling their way towards the corridor light bulb in the same slow purposeful way as sea anemones.

Then, apparently losing interest in the bulb, her hair dragged Rachel haltingly along the corridor. Occasionally she lingered long enough for a tuft to explore the complex whorls on the ceiling.

When she passed Eric's room, Morpeth tapped with the edges of his nails, not expecting an answer – but the door sprang wide at once. Eric stood there in his pyjamas, his hands covering the mouths of the prapsies. They fidgeted in his grasp, necks craned wildly, trying to get a good look at Rachel.

'Were you awake?' Morpeth whispered.

'Nope, until these two started bouncing off the walls.' Eric blinked, adjusting to the pre-dawn light. 'What's up?'

'Keep quiet and follow me,' said Morpeth. 'And leave the boys here.'

'Oh, Morpeth—'

'No. Come alone.'

Reluctantly Eric tucked the prapsies back under the quilt of his bed, resting their heads together on a pillow. Their eyes followed him mournfully.

'Please, Eric,' one pleaded. 'Let us come. We are so quiet. Watch.' It opened and closed its mouth silently.

The other prapsy giggled. 'You look like a guppy fish!'

'Shut up. Eric was believing me!'

'Sorry, boys,' Eric said, petting their neck feathers. 'Next time, maybe.'

He drew the bedroom door rapidly shut. Moments later the prapsies pressed their lips to the crack at the bottom. They began a low whine, like abandoned puppies.

Eric caught up with Morpeth at the bottom of the staircase.

'Blimey,' he said, spotting Rachel. 'What a sight! Is her hair alive or something? And where's she going?' He half-laughed as she passed the bathroom. 'The loo?'

'Shush. You'll see,' said Morpeth. 'Keep a close eye on her. I might need your help if things go wrong.'

Rachel entered the kitchen, making her way to the patio doors leading to the garden.

'It's locked,' said Eric. 'She'll never get out there.'

'She's more resourceful than you realize,' said Morpeth.

Eric heard a subtle click as the patio locks were disengaged without the use of a key.

'Impressive,' he said.

'Not really,' Morpeth answered. 'Locks are designed to be unlocked. For Rachel, this level of magic isn't even a challenge.'

The doors of the patio snapped forcefully open and Rachel glided into the garden. Her eyes remained closed as she came to a standing rest in the middle of the lawn. Then, twisting her head, she sniffed the late night air – and a sudden, distinctive aroma of many flowers struck Eric. The smell was rich and impossibly, overwhelmingly, strong.

'What's she doing?' Eric gasped.

Morpeth laughed. 'I don't know. There are no rules here, or only ones her spells make up. What happens next depends on whose turn it is.'

'You're joking,' said Eric. 'The spells take turns?'

'You'll see.'

Rachel, her eyes still shut tight, began to fly in rapid circles around the garden. With outstretched arms her hands touched everything: grass, leaves, the grain of the wooden fence, the silkiness of petals, the hardness of rose-thorns. She stopped, knelt, tasting the moisture on the grass and the damp acrid soil beneath. She sighed as she pressed her cheek against the toughest flints in the rock garden. She caught a moth and stroked it, deep and long across its fragile wings.

'I've seen this from her before,' said Morpeth, 'Her spells apparently enjoy the contrasts. Sharp and smooth, sour and sweet. She gets a pleasure from them I can't understand.'

'I wouldn't want to be that moth,' said Eric.

'She won't hurt it,' Morpeth assured him. 'If the moth struggles Rachel can somehow hold the delicate wings without damaging them.'

Rachel opened her hand, and the uninjured moth flapped confusedly away. She half-chased it, flapping her ears in imitation, but the insect was clearly too dull to interest her spells for long. She forgot it. She lifted her chin and raised her arms, soaring gracefully moonwards. Within seconds she was just a dwindling point of yellow nightdress against its scarred white disc.

'Flipping heck!' said Eric. 'Are you telling me she's still asleep?'

'Not just asleep,' Morpeth told him. 'It's much deeper than that – a slumber, compelled by her spells. Rachel herself has no control over any of this.'

'It sounds dangerous,' Eric said, staring up with concern. 'Should we wake her? I could destroy the spells keeping her asleep.'

Morpeth looked surprised. 'Can you actually trace the spells doing that?'

Eric nodded. 'Yeah. All spells have their own special smell. I learned that on Ithrea. The ones she's using a lot tonight, like the flying spells, are easy to recognize after a while. Rarer spells are trickier, but I can usually work them out eventually.' He licked his finger and grinned. 'Of course, once I destroy a spell that person can't use it again, so I have to be careful.' He squinted at Rachel's tiny speck body. 'I can't reach her from here, though. She's too far away.'

A dot of gleaming yellow casually sank from the sky. As Rachel alighted on the lawn her nightdress rose and settled smoothly over her knees.

'What next?' Eric wondered.

'Who knows,' said Morpeth, looking worried. 'It's always something unexpected, but her spells are especially lively tonight.'

Rachel altered her shape. It occurred instantly, not gradually. At first Eric thought she had vanished; then he noticed whiskers in the grass, quivering on a petite black nose: a field mouse.

'She's shape-changed!' marvelled Eric. 'I saw that on Ithrea, but I've never seen her do it here. Isn't it risky?'

'Rachel's spells wouldn't do anything to harm her,' said Morpeth. 'However, the cat might need to be careful.'

'The cat?'

Sophie, the family tabby, had uncurled herself from a comfy doze somewhere in the house. Drawn by a sudden tasty scent of rodent, she crouched low in the grass and deftly stalked her victim. When she was close enough to pounce, she waited for the mouse to run. It merely twitched its whiskers – and Sophie almost leapt out of the garden.

A *hundred* mice had appeared on the lawn, all squeaking Sophie's name.

As she sprang away the mice vanished with a giggle. Sophie, her fur on end, remained perfectly still for a while. Finally she returned languidly to the kitchen, settled herself on the floor and began primly cleaning her claws as if nothing had taken place.

'This is brilliant,' Eric said. 'Didn't realize Rach had a sense of humour. What next? A giant prapsy?'

Rachel had reverted to normal. She hovered for a few minutes above the ground. While her bare toes tickled the dewy grass, her head became unnaturally still, cocked slightly to one side – as if listening to the stars.

Then she disappeared altogether.

'She's *shifted*!' said Eric. 'Wow! One place to another.' Behind him, there was a rustle. He turned, expecting it to be Rachel. 'Oh no,' he muttered. 'We're for it now.'

Mum walked purposefully across the garden in her slippers and dressing gown.

'Well?' she asked, staring at Morpeth.

'Mostly the usual pattern,' he answered. 'But the mouse

trick is new, and Rachel's rarely gone so far from the house before. Her flying spells are really active.'

Mum nodded grimly. 'Two days ago just whizzing around the block seemed to keep them happy. Not any more, obviously. I've been viewing her from the window. Never seen such crazy stunts. I don't know how fast she's flying. I couldn't follow her.'

Eric gaped. 'You've been watching her, Mum?'

'Of course,' she replied matter-of-factly. 'Ever since this all started. Do you think either of you could leave the house without me noticing? I worked out the meaning of that pond smell long before Morpeth. Since then we've been taking it in turns to keep an eye on her.' She buttoned up Eric's pyjama top. 'It's chilly out here. Imagine how cold Rachel must be up – ' she flung her arms – 'wherever she is out there.'

'She won't feel it,' said Morpeth. 'Her spells will keep her warm.'

'She's back,' said Eric, 'with a weird thing in her hair.'

An exotic, long-stemmed plant, nestled in Rachel's fringe. In the lightening sky they could just make out its unusual green and red-brown flowers.

Mum's gaze narrowed. 'That's an orchid. I recognize it … a Frog Orchid, it's called. They don't grow in this country. Spain, I think. Surely Rachel can't have gone that far?'

'If she shifted she could have gone anywhere,' Morpeth said.

Rachel plucked the orchid from her hair and longingly tasted its dainty petals.

Mum's voice became suddenly exasperated. 'I hate what that Wizard did to her,' she said. 'What kind of gift is it that allows Rachel to keep her magic, but not use it? Those spells of hers – playing games, fighting for control, using her. How can they be a gift? They're nothing but a curse, a worry for us all.'

'Docile little spells wouldn't be much use against Witches,' Morpeth told her. 'Larpskendya knew Rachel would need all her magic if she ever faced them.' He followed Rachel's tongue as it became a skinny tube that delicately probed the heart of the orchid flower. Her face was blissful. 'But I wonder if Larpskendya predicted Rachel's spells would behave quite like this,' Morpeth said earnestly. 'They're so suddenly, desperately alive, after being so quiet. Has there been a change? Something Larpskendya didn't anticipate?'

'Is there *anything* she can't do?' Mum asked Morpeth.

'I don't understand her limits,' he admitted. 'Neither does Rachel. On Ithrea she only had a few days to learn, and because of her promise to Larpskendya she hasn't experimented with her magic at all since she came back.' He watched wistfully as Rachel breathed on a clenched rosebud. It opened up its petals to her mouth as if she had offered a gift of sunlight. 'She's without doubt the most naturally gifted child I ever met,' Morpeth continued. 'On Ithrea Rachel learned to perform spells others took centuries to discover or never achieved. She did them without being taught, instinctively altering shape or shifting effortlessly between locations, or commanding the weather. No child had ever done such things; only the Witch, Dragwena.'

'You were pretty impressive yourself on Ithrea,' Eric pointed out,

'Not really,' Morpeth said. 'I could heal basic injuries. With difficulty I could change the shape of some materials, send signals. Of course, even that simple level of magic is beyond a lot of children.'

'Don't you miss it?' Eric asked hesitantly. 'I mean, you must hate Larpskendya for taking away your magic.'

'No, Eric, you're wrong,' Morpeth replied. 'I *asked* Larpskendya to remove it.'

'What?' Eric gasped. 'Why?'

'We daren't attract the attention of the Witches. I've used magic for so long that a spell is bound to slip out accidentally at some point. So I asked Larpskendya to take it from me shortly after returning to Earth – and he did.'

'I never knew that,' Mum said softly. 'You never told us.'

'It wasn't as big a sacrifice as you think,' Morpeth said, smiling crookedly. 'I'm an old man. Unlike Rachel's, my magic these last years was mostly content to snooze.'

That's not true, Mum realized, studying his face. You just didn't want Rachel worrying about you; that's why you didn't tell us.

Rachel sat cross-legged near the pond, her eyes still closed. As they watched, her cheeks swelled with cold morning air. When she exhaled the air in the garden immediately became tropical, and they breathed in the diverse, humid scents of a rainforest.

Then, without warning, Rachel dived into the pond.

'Shield your eyes!' Morpeth cried.

Eric half-heartedly lifted an arm. 'What's wrong? I don't—'

'Do it!'

Mum just had time to cover his face with a hand before extremely bright light flooded the garden. It was not the light of dawn. It came from Rachel. At last she had opened her night eyes. In sunshine the spell-colours varied, but in darkness they glittered one dazzling colour only – clear silver. For a moment opals of light swept across Mum, Eric and Morpeth, illuminating their clothes. Then Rachel settled back in the pond and set her gaze on the sky. Clouds, thousands of feet in the air, were lit up, pierced by the miniature searchbeams. The pond enlarged slightly to welcome her. She lay in the deepest part, and red gills appeared on her neck.

'That's new,' said Morpeth, peering cautiously between his fingers.

A third gill had materialized, this time on her throat.

Rachel lay in the pond, her mouth open under the water. As the others anxiously watched, her magic-skilful eyes scanned the skies for sights they could never have detected. Within minutes, their blazing silver light had attracted legions of moths and flies from the surrounding gardens and beyond.

Eventually Rachel emerged serenely from the pond. She floated back to her room, never once showing any recognition of her family. Eric was sent back to bed. For a while there were shrieks of excitement from his room as he told the prapsies what had happened. Downstairs there were only soft murmurings, as Morpeth sat with Mum and together they discussed what should be done.

Later that morning Morpeth had to shake Rachel repeatedly to wake her. Her eyes, when they finally opened, were bleary grey, like a summary of winter.

'I'm so tired,' she said, gazing in the mirror. Rubbing her face, she sensed the contentment of her spells. Most of them hung back from her eyes, seemingly satisfied, not pestering her to play.

'Last night's games took a heavy toll,' Morpeth said, explaining what had occurred.

Listening to the events, Rachel muttered angrily, 'You'd think my own spells hate me, the things they do…'

Morpeth gripped her shoulders. 'It's not that. They're just so fierce. There's a wildness about your magic I only ever saw in Dragwena. It yearns to be used.'

Rachel glanced uneasily at the saturated sheets. 'Mum can't have missed this. She knows, doesn't she?'

'Yes, your mum knows everything.'

'Oh, that's just *great*.'

'No, it's good news,' Morpeth said firmly. 'We need everyone's strength now.'

Rachel showered, dressed and made her way downstairs to a strangely silent kitchen. Even the prapsies were quiet. 'What's the matter with them?' she asked Eric suspiciously, pouring out a bowl of cereal. 'Are they sick or something?'

Eric raised his eyebrows. 'No. The boys have new respect for you, Rach. They saw you flying through the bedroom curtains. No more insults for a couple of days. They insist!'

The prapsies beamed at Rachel, flapping their wings and winking knowingly.

When they had finished breakfast and were all in the living room, Rachel said, 'I noticed something strange last night. It scared me, and I'm not sure what it means.' She sat on the edge of the couch, close to Mum. 'My information spells picked it up. You know the way they automatically record everything going on around me, whether I'm interested or not. It's usually just pointless junk, who's in the house, what's their heart-rate, the time the sun came up, pointless stuff like that. Last night, though, they went out a long way and picked up signs of magic. It wasn't mine. The magic belonged to other children. Thousands of them.'

The prapsies stopped prancing on the radiator.

'I thought Larpskendya wouldn't allow that,' said Eric. 'Didn't he say it was too dangerous to let the magic of children loose?'

'Yes, he did. He never normally interferes in the natural way magic wants to develop, but Earth is different. Larpskendya told me it's a special case, because of Dragwena. She was here for centuries before the Wizards discovered us, breeding her own kind of magic in children. Due to her, Larpskendya says, there's a streak of Witch in us all.'

'Ugh!' said Eric.

Rachel nodded. 'Larpskendya wanted to keep watch over us, not releasing our magic until he was sure it was safe.' She glanced at Morpeth. 'Larpskendya's not close,' she said, with certainty. 'He can't be; otherwise he would have warned us about something this important.'

'I agree,' said Morpeth. 'Try sending him a message.'

Rachel transmitted a distress call in all directions in the way Larpskendya had shown her.

'No answer,' she said, after a few minutes.

'What does that mean?' Eric asked. 'Larpskendya's not … hurt is he?'

'Don't be stupid,' Rachel snapped, the idea unbearable. 'It just means … he's not close, that's all.' She lodged the calling spell in her mind, ensuring that it would be sent accurately and far into deepest space whether she was awake or asleep. 'Larpskendya said he couldn't always be here,' she reminded Eric. 'We're not the only world he has to look out for.' But what, she wondered, could have been so urgent that Larpskendya didn't have time to warn us he was leaving?

'Well,' said Morpeth, 'for the time being we have to decide what to do ourselves. Tell me, Rachel, are any of the children your spells detected actively using their magic yet?'

'I don't think so,' she replied. 'But in the most gifted it's almost bursting to get out.'

'How far did you search?'

'Halfway across the world. It's the same pattern every-where. And there was something really odd, Morpeth. A trace over Africa. So far away, but I've never felt anything that sharp.'

'What now, then?' Eric asked.

'We prepare ourselves as best we can,' said Morpeth, matter-of-factly. 'If levels of magic are so high, anything could be about to happen.' He turned to Rachel. 'This recent flowering of magic might explain why your spells have become so headstrong lately. I saw something similar occasionally on Ithrea: the magic of certain extremely gifted children reaching out, wanting to be together. Maybe that's why your spells have been so busy recently. They sense friends out there, almost ready to welcome. Spells enjoy companionship, too.' He held her gaze. 'We should start with a vigorous daily practice routine for your magic. That should satisfy those lively spells of yours. It might even put an end to their night-time adventures.'

Rachel nodded fervently – and the moment she did so, the moment she accepted that she must open herself fully to the entire richness of her magic – a wealth of fresh colours burst into her eyes. The colours came from dozens of spells new to her. These were small spells, minor spells, useful for particular occasions. They had quiet, almost shy, voices that rarely challenged the dominance of the major spells like the flyers and shifters. Now that she had at last noticed them, Rachel invited the spells forward. Respectfully, she asked each to identify itself for the first time, and they – in their mild, reserved way – tiptoed into her mind.

'Are you sure you know what you're doing, Rachel?' Mum asked anxiously, seeing the new soft pastel shades.

'No,' Rachel answered. 'I'm not sure about anything. But Morpeth's right: I've let some of my spells do what they want for too long.' She smiled. 'Safety first. We don't want any prying eyes, do we?'

She placed a blanketing spell around the house to prevent any magic seeping out.

Then she stared into the garden. She looked at the pond whose dank water she had swallowed over so many nights. She looked at the garden fence, shredded in places where her cheeks had rubbed against the surface. And she thought about Nigeria, in Africa, and the abundance of magic her information spells had sensed there.

'It's time to get my body back,' she said to Mum. 'No more dips in the pond. And from now on, if I fly someplace it's because I choose to go there. We'll start practising right now.'

4

the camberwell beauty

Dawn, and sleepy African birds were waking, as Fola trudged along the path from Fiditi to the river.

With one hand she reached over her head, expertly re-balancing the heavy weight of the washing basket. With the other she adjusted her *oja*. It made little difference: Yemi, her baby brother, was an awkward lump on her back no matter how she carried him – he would not stop moving and kicking!

'Be quiet! Stay still!' she said irritably. The tiniest things excited him: a bird doing nothing in a tree, a dog moping on the path, even the small plumes of dust thrown up by her feet.

Only a baby could enjoy such a tedious walk, Fola thought.

Absently she gazed ahead. In front, clear and boisterous, the Odooba river sliced through the forest. Fola knew from school how it cut a path between villages in southern Nigeria on its way down to the sea, but such details didn't interest her. She had seen its waters so often that she hardly noticed them. Reaching the bank she gratefully unloaded Yemi and the washing and stretched her aching neck muscles.

It was early, and still cool, but she was already tired. She had woken before dawn to prepare the yams and black-eye beans for the evening meal. There was still work to finish when she got back, and Yemi to mind all day. Fola did not complain. With Baba hunting in the rainforest, she was happy to help out. It was easier than Mama's day in the fields – long hours of hard work.

A few other girls from the village had already arrived at the river. Fola greeted them warmly as she wet the soda soap and doused the clothes.

While she worked Yemi sat in a sort of comfortable heap by her feet. He sifted dust. He blinked at midges circling his close-cropped hair. He saw a brown-black Asa hawk. It waved its big wings and he waved back.

Fola made sure that he was not too close to the river's edge, and engaged in the usual gossip with the other girls. A short while later she heard a sharp intake of breath. She turned to find Yemi sitting abnormally still.

'What is it?' she said. 'What incredible wonder have you discovered this time?'

It was a fly, and it had landed on Yemi's bare forearm.

He stared in awe, mouth wide, as the fly crawled towards his elbow.

Then, without even a friendly wave, the fly flew off.

Yemi started to cry. He covered his face and tears streamed out.

'Oh, don't be silly,' said Fola. She put down the skirt she was wringing out and picked him up. 'It's only a fly. You can't *make* them stay, you know!'

When Yemi continued to snuffle she rummaged for his special book. It was a pop-up book filled with pictures of butterflies. Yemi forgot the fly at once, stopped crying and reached out eagerly. Fola sat with him for a few minutes, helping him turn the pages. He stopped her, as always, at the page containing his favourite butterfly.

It was a Mourning Cloak, otherwise called a Camberwell Beauty. According to the book they came in many colours. The illustration showed a lovely bright yellow variety, with small patches of light brown dusting its wings.

'Want,' Yemi told her.

'Do you?' Fola said, amused.

He kissed the image of the Camberwell Beauty ardently.

'We don't have that kind in Africa,' she informed him. 'It comes from far away. We will never see one here.'

Yemi's face crumpled with sadness. He looked so unhappy that Fola spent longer than she should have done reading with him. When she returned to the washing Yemi flipped the pages back to his Camberwell Beauty. He studied it and frowned.

Fola took over an hour to complete the washing, beating the sheets and laying them out in the rising sun. When the last of the linen was nearly dry, she searched around for Yemi. He sat close by, still reading his book.

And he had a new companion – a yellow butterfly.

It was perched on Yemi's forearm precisely where the fly had been.

Fola blinked. There was no doubt it was a Camberwell Beauty.

Yemi grinned from ear to ear. He blew on his arm and the butterfly started fanning him. He wriggled his nose and it hopped on the tip. Then, slowly, like a ballerina, it rotated on spindly black legs until it faced Fola – and bowed.

She dropped the washing.

Sitting heavily down she noticed other flapping movements all around. Many more Camberwell Beauties were alighting from the northern sky onto the grass and soil surrounding Yemi. As Fola watched they all fluttered onto his right shoulder. Clambering on top of one another, they formed a neat pyramid. Yemi leafed through his picture book. Streaking light from the early sun reflected from the pages, making them difficult to read. Yemi squinted, then laughed. He glanced at his butterflies.

Instantly all their delicate wings opened, casting the pages in yellow shadow.

5

fish without
armour

Heebra's Witches were famished when they reached Earth. The journey had taken far longer than she had expected. Exhausted, their hungry soul-snakes shrivelled against their breasts, the scouting party only endured the final stretch because she drove them.

Yet here, at last, was the great prize: Rachel's home planet.

Despite their craving for food, Heebra held the Witches back – she needed to be certain there were no Wizards. Cautiously she circled the planet with two scouts. Larpskendya's unmistakable stink was everywhere – but his scent was old, and there were no other Wizards present.

Excellent. It meant the Gridda warriors were distracting well in far-flung places.

Shrieking with anticipation the Witches plunged towards the sunlit half of the world. A few defence satellites swivelled, registering their presence. Heebra easily damped the primitive electronic messages and, undetected, the Witches swept into the thermosphere. For a moment its hot layer held them up; then they adjusted their body shapes so that the searing heat merely sloughed off the useless dead layers of space-skin. Joyfully they emerged into the upper atmosphere, shuddering with rapture as coldness splashed across their new raw flesh.

'Feast! Feast!' Heebra ordered her starving Witches.

They dived through the swirling blue and white cloud. Into the deeps of the Pacific Ocean they sank, feeding on skipjack tuna and the great white sharks that hunt them.

However, this ocean was too warm for the Witches' liking, so they moved north. Swimming amongst the ice-floes of the Arctic they gorged on vast schools of herring.

'No weapons,' Calen marvelled, studying the fish. 'Unlike those on Ool, they simply gather in dumb shoals, apparently waiting to be eaten. Where is their armour and poison? I hope we find something more interesting to test us soon.'

But the largest creatures they could find were killer whales. These fled when the Witches tried to stimulate a fight. Heebra hastily drew the Witches towards land before they became too bored. She made base close to the North Pole. Here polar bear and oily seal flesh was rich and plentiful and concealment required only the simplest of spells. The temperature was too mild, but the occasional blizzards blew fresh and clear: a reminder of home. Within hours the Witches were already clawing at the frozen rock below the snows, energetically building the bases of new eye-towers.

Once they were settled, Heebra dispatched her five scouts. Across the globe the Witches probed, disguised in many forms, mastering the simple structure of the languages – and studying children everywhere. All the scout reports fascinated Heebra.

Calen was the last to return. Several hours after the others arrived Heebra saw her black dress rippling in the distance. Calen flew in typically flamboyant manner, bald head cutting through the wind, scudding low across the snow. She pressed her arms sleekly to the sides of her body, using only the tips of her claws to change direction.

'Well?' Heebra asked impatiently, as she alighted.

Calen transformed her face into a young boy she had recently met, indicating the tiny milk teeth.

'These children have nothing to scare us!'

'Obviously,' said Heebra. 'The other Witches are full of contempt. How do you judge them?'

'Where do I start? They're so weak. Frail liquid eyes, with no night vision or x-ray. They bleed at the slightest cut.' Calen laughed. 'Their skin *tears* – can you believe that! And soft internal organs, unshielded. That makes them vulnerable. They are also prone to endless disease and infections. And slow, Mother. Slow to react, think, move or sense danger. Nothing recommends them.' She tapped her skull. 'Above their brains is a fibrous hair-scalp growth. It ignites at the least touch – a ridiculous evolution!'

'Did you expect something more impressive?' Heebra asked.

'Didn't you?'

Heebra raked Mak's scales. 'Open your eyes. Their bodies may be flimsy, but this species are natural killers. Wars between them are happening everywhere on this planet. We have rarely known such a promising race. I see signs of Dragwena's healthy influence everywhere.'

'It's such a pity we can't use the adults,' sighed Calen. 'The magic they have as children decays early.'

'What do you think of their technology?'

'It's no danger to us,' scoffed Calen. 'A poor substitute for magic. They can't even detect our presence.'

'Agreed. We must concentrate on the children. Assess their magic.'

'Larpskendya is clearly interfering, holding them back,' said Calen. 'His influence has led to some peculiar features, such as child schooling. Instead of being free to practise their spells, the young ones sit behind desks, obeying the adults. How wasteful!'

'Larpskendya never usually influences the development path of magic on any world,' mused Heebra. 'Tell me why this planet is different.' She glared threateningly at Nylo who, remembering the last time Heebra had held him, hid his blunt head inside Calen's dress.

'These children have little discipline,' Calen replied warily. 'The youngest behave instinctively, seizing what they can – remarkably like our own kind. Larpskendya must fear that if he unleashes their magic the children could start along a destructive path.'

'Starting with the removal of the inferior adults,' agreed Heebra. 'Followed by a battle amongst the children themselves as the best learn to dominate.'

Calen smiled. 'How Larpskendya would hate that! It would be good to watch.'

'Can the children be used against the Wizards themselves?'

'Yes, they *will* fight for us,' Calen answered confidently. 'Their magic is brimming, and the simplest of spells is required to free it. We can train them as we would our own student-witches.' She laughed. 'We'll soon have them despising the adults. Larpskendya has the children so mixed up. Can you believe that when they injure an opponent they often feel guilt?'

'No matter how well we train them, no child could ever defeat a Wizard,' said Heebra.

'True, but these children like to be together, Mother. We could form them into large packs, give them a purpose. They would enjoy that. A hundred, perhaps, could distract a Wizard for long enough for us to finish him off. And there are so many of the little things. We could waste millions and not run out!'

'I wonder,' Heebra said thoughtfully. 'I have studied these children myself. They are contrary, often stubborn, and less predictable than you think. A few will resist us strongly; others will be difficult to master. The Rachel child is evidence enough. Dragwena obviously tried to train her, but somehow the girl held out. Remarkable: to resist a High Witch. No creature except a Wizard has ever done that.'

Calen shrugged. 'Rachel is probably unique. A single, extraordinary child.'

'Possibly,' said Heebra. 'I doubt it. On such a large world there may be many extraordinary children. And magic on this world is raw. Who knows how it will evolve?'

Calen said defiantly, 'In all our history of conquering, this is the first time we have discovered a species like these. What have we left to fight the Wizards? Larpskendya drives us back in humiliation closer to Ool every year. Is that what you want, Mother? An undignified death defending your own eye-tower from Larpskendya? Is his name to be whispered in awe amongst us forever?'

'*I* will decide what should be done,' growled Heebra.

Raising her muscular bare arms she glided into a bank of high clouds. For a while Heebra simply drifted amidst the polar winds, finding their touch pleasantly cool. A nest of spiders crept to the front of her jaws to feel the frost, and look out at the recently completed eye-towers of the Witches. The familiar sight elated the spiders, and Heebra licked them indulgently.

'Here are my instructions,' she said, flying back to Calen. 'Focus your training on the youngest. They are the most easily persuaded. Ignore all except the most gifted children or the most ruthless. Where you can set children against adults – parents, teachers, any others who regulate behaviour – do so. The most important thing is to work fast. Discover leaders, Calen. We can't train all the children ourselves. Find me those who will push and punish their own kind.'

Calen's tattoos sparkled with excitement. She started to leave, then turned back. 'You mention nothing of Rachel, or Eric. Surely you want revenge?'

'I haven't forgotten them,' said Heebra. 'Briefly I sought Rachel out myself. She was not difficult to find. Despite her efforts to hide her gifts, the quality of her magic blazes like a beacon on this small world.'

'What do you make of her?' Calen asked with interest.

'A startling member of her species. I can see why Larpskendya is so interested in her. And she has an unusual gift we can use.'

'A gift?'

'She has a direct connection with Larpskendya himself.'

Calen gasped, knowing how long the Witches had sought such a way to lead them to Larpskendya. 'Can we use this to locate him directly?' she asked.

'No, Larpskendya obscures the path back to him. But if we use the link carefully we might be able to use it to draw him to *us*.'

'Is Rachel calling for Larpskendya now?' asked Calen. 'We would not want him to arrive before we are prepared.'

'She calls him, of course she does!' laughed Heebra. 'Bewildered, confused Rachel – she is frantically sending out her signal. However, Larpskendya hears nothing. I've placed about her a damping spell the girl will never find.'

'When will you release it?'

'When we have trained enough children. When we are settled and I have decided how to set a trap for

Larpskendya. Until then he will get no warnings from Rachel. He will come when we are ready for *him*.'

Calen nodded. 'When the time is right do you intend to kill Rachel yourself?'

'She is hardly worth my attention,' answered Heebra. 'I have been thinking about a more interesting way to deal with her.' She poked a claw at Calen. 'You set much faith in the youngsters on this world, so I set you this task: find me another child capable of challenging Rachel. Find and train an executioner from her own species. Rachel's death will be so much more satisfying that way.'

'I may have already found such a child,' said Calen brightly. 'She is unusual in every way. I'll show her to you soon. A surprise!'

While Calen left to give the other Witches their orders, Heebra drifted for a few minutes longer in the polar winds, opening up her jaws. The spiders within rolled around, delighting in the direct touch of snowflakes.

Heebra dropped to the ground. A nearby polar bear raised its muzzle from the snow, wandered across and licked her feet. Heebra rolled with it playfully, tumbling over and over, careful not to injure the bear's thin hide with her claws.

Well, she thought; well now, Larpskendya. This world is your worst nightmare, isn't it? How these children must fill you with dread. I see why you have enslaved their magic, kept this world such a carefully guarded secret. You are afraid, aren't you? You are afraid because more than any other species these children are like *us*!

6

the hairy fly

Mum scooped porridge oats into Eric's breakfast bowl.

'More, please,' he said.

She crammed on one more dollop. 'Enough?'

'A bit more.'

Somehow she balanced two more spoonfuls on top of the porridge mountain.

'Surely that's enough…'

'Just a *little* bit more.'

Morpeth lounged nearby. 'It's already spilling over the plate,' he muttered. 'How are you going to eat all that?'

Eric picked up his spoon. 'I'm growing. I *need* this food, unlike some with the appetite' – he pulled a face at Rachel, sitting opposite – 'of an ant.'

'You want it for the prapsies,' Rachel said matter-of-factly. 'I've seen them slurping from your dish.' She laughed and sucked in her lips. 'They get it all over their faces.'

Mum sighed deeply. 'Eric, is that true?'

'Er...'

'No, don't tell me,' Mum said. 'I'd rather not know...' She picked up her handbag and a light coat. 'I'm popping out for about an hour – the mobile's on if you need me.' She stared at Eric. 'There had better not be any porridge in unusual places in my kitchen when I get back. Understood?' Eric nodded and she left the house.

A few minutes later Rachel noticed a commotion by the kitchen window.

'What's bothering the boys?' she asked.

Both prapsies were jabbering wildly, flying in tight spirals, too excited to speak. When everyone rushed over one finally found its voice.

'A big shaggy marvel!' it cried, peering through the lace curtains.

'A flying yowler!' the other said.

'Rubbish! A hairy fly!'

Eric blinked at the sun. 'Blimey.'

High in the pure blue sky, flying over the rooftops, a black shape turned smooth circles. 'Looks like a dog,' Eric said. 'That's ridiculous. It must be a kite.'

'No strings,' Morpeth said. 'And it's barking!'

'A Labrador,' whispered Rachel.

Eric nudged her. 'What's going on? Are *you* doing this?'

'Of course not.'

'Then who is?'

54

The Labrador was suspended in mid-air over the centre of a playing field. It lay on its back, big paws paddling the sky. Then it yelped, spun around, and shot straight upwards. Some boys, kicking a football around the field, didn't know whether to watch or run.

'Flipping heck,' Eric said. 'It's controlled by a spell. Magic, Rachel!'

She nodded, trembling slightly, trying to pinpoint the source, and calling to mind the defensive spells she had practised over the past couple of weeks.

The prapsies panted in Eric's ears.

'I could destroy the spell if you want,' he said.

'No,' Rachel answered. 'The dog's too high up. We'd injure it.'

'Why not use your own magic, Rach?'

'Not yet,' warned Morpeth. 'Don't reveal yourself until we understand what we're up against. Let's get to the field.'

They raced out of the house. The prapsies squeezed past Eric's shoulder before he could shut the door.

'Hey, come back, boys!' he called. 'You're not allowed out!'

The prapsies flew jubilantly over the houses and soon caught the dog. Chatting excitedly, they copied its stormy movements across the sky.

'Hey, come back!' one prapsy wailed into the Labrador's ear.

'Naughty dog!' the other cried. 'Quiet down, you shaggy wonder!'

Rachel led the way up the steeply rising streets towards

the field. As they approached, the dog's body started making new patterns in the air – long rhythmical shapes – a mixture of loops and straight lines.

Eric struggled to keep up with Rachel's long strides. 'It's flipping possessed!'

'No,' said Morpeth, tracing the dog's movements. 'It's a name.'

'What's a name?'

They arrived at the bottom of the field.

'That is.' Morpeth pointed at the sky. 'PAUL. Can't you see? The dog's writing the same name over and over again.'

They hurried to the top of the field, until they were directly under the frantic Labrador. The soccer boys had scarpered, leaving their ball behind.

'We're close enough,' Rachel said. 'Bring it down, Eric.'

Eric pointed his finger at the Labrador, putting an end to the flying spell, and the dog dropped from the sky. Just before it reached the ground Rachel spread a cushioning spell on the grass. The dog landed safely on all fours and fled down the hill, barking at the top of its voice. The prapsies pursued it gleefully, offering useless advice.

'Paul,' mused Eric. 'That doesn't sound like a dog's name.'

'No,' said Rachel. 'I think it belongs to *him*.'

She pointed to the bottom of the field. There, half-hidden in the thick grass, lay a plump spiky-haired boy about the same age as Eric. Propped on his elbows he was concentrating furiously on the dog, flicking his fingers, as if trying to send the Labrador back into the air.

Eric grinned. 'He can't do it. He doesn't understand that after I destroy a spell he can never get it to work again.'

'Stay back,' Morpeth said. 'Let him make the next move.'

Eric squinted. 'What's he doing now? He's looking at that ball.'

The leather football rose a few inches in the air, then slid low across the grass. It moved much faster than it could ever have been kicked.

'It's heading for us,' Morpeth remarked.

'Actually,' Rachel said, 'it's heading for me.'

The ball gathered pace, rising to the level of her head, a swift blur.

Eric jabbed his finger, destroying the spell, but the ball's momentum was so great that it continued to aim straight at Rachel. She made it swerve harmlessly around her shoulders.

'He did that deliberately,' Eric fumed. 'Let's get him!'

Rachel shook her head. 'No. Let's see what he does next.'

The spiky-haired boy frowned. The next moment Rachel felt a new spell, this time working on her.

'I can't believe it,' she said. 'He's trying to shove my face in the dirt.'

'Let me squash the spell,' Eric growled. Rachel gestured no, trying to understand something about the boy's magic.

'He seems inexperienced,' Morpeth said to her. 'Do you sense any real authority or subtlety about his spells?'

'No,' she replied, watching the boy anxiously repeat the same spell again. 'Just raw ability, freshly awakened – and powerful.'

'But why is he trying to hurt you, or that dog?' Eric asked.

Rachel was uncertain. Had this boy really tried to harm her and the Labrador? Or was he merely testing his own magic, and hers, curious about what they could both do?

They tentatively stepped towards Paul. When Morpeth was close enough to see his face, he noticed how frightened the boy looked. He gasped and juddered, his body jerking first towards Rachel, then away. Finally he sprinted off down the path.

'Come on,' Eric said. 'He can't escape that way. Hey, Rach, you could fly after him.'

'No,' she said. 'I don't want to show him what I can do yet.'

They followed the path to the bottom of the hill, where it curved sharply into a large flat meadow. The meadow was empty.

'Where is he?' gasped Eric. 'There's nowhere to hide. How could he have run away that fast?'

'He didn't outrun us,' said Morpeth. 'He must have waited until he got out of sight, then found a *different* way out of the meadow. Could he have flown?'

'No,' said Rachel, her face pale. 'It's not that. Someone or *something* else whisked Paul away. I felt a brief trace of magic, unlike the boy's. It was incredibly strong.' She sent information spells out for over a mile. All signs of Paul had gone. 'I can't detect anything. The trail ends here.' She dropped to her knees, where a single shoeprint of flattened grass marked the last place Paul had stood. Already the grass was springing back into place, as if he had never existed.

'Do you think Paul could have performed this vanishing act himself?' she asked Morpeth.

'I doubt it,' he said thoughtfully. 'Not so perfectly. It takes great skill to seal off tracks made by recent spells – and that boy was flustered. He must have had help – and from someone much more experienced.'

As they walked back home, Eric snarled, 'Whatever's going on I don't like this Paul. You saw what he did. Deliberately scaring that dog, and enjoying it.'

Morpeth rubbed his chin. 'Was he enjoying it? That's not what I noticed. I saw a boy at odds, either with himself or an invisible companion. Something was scaring him.'

As they arrived at the front gate the prapsies landed on Eric's shoulders. They noisily spat out dog hairs.

Rachel winced. 'They didn't bite the Labrador, did they?'

'Nah.' Eric pulled a face. 'Probably got that way trying to kiss it.'

He tucked the prapsies into his shirt before anyone on the street could see their flushed happy faces.

Morpeth guided them into the living room, relieved that Mum had not yet returned. For a few minutes they scanned the doors and windows, half expecting a rage-filled Paul to smash his way through.

'I thought you told us no kids could use their magic yet,' Eric said to Rachel. 'What's going on?'

Rachel trembled slightly, turning to Morpeth. 'Do you understand this?'

He shrugged. 'Something must have sparked off Paul's magic. Almost anything could have triggered it. An emotion, perhaps – anger or fear.' He thought of Ithrea: a favourite tactic of Dragwena, he remembered, was to panic children into releasing their spells.

'Do you think Paul's the only kid out there using magic?' Eric asked.

'Possibly. I doubt it,' Morpeth said. 'Or not for long. Whatever's caused this, we should assume that Paul is just the beginning. Hundreds of children may soon be spell-making.' He glanced at Rachel. 'Larpskendya never intended or wanted this, I'm sure. It confirms that he can't be close.'

We *are* on our own, Rachel realized. She fought against that idea, and noticed her spells withdrawing deep within her.

'I don't much fancy the idea of kids with magic,' Eric muttered. 'Imagine a bully who could use a blinding spell!'

'If enough children can use magic, we might have to prepare for worse than that,' Morpeth said gravely. 'On Ithrea, I saw all kinds of children arrive over the centuries. The strongest-minded resisted Dragwena's influence for a while, but some' – he paused – 'well, let's say some didn't try hard. They willingly directed their magic against other children. A few didn't even need Dragwena's encouragement. They enjoyed it.'

Rachel shuddered. 'Think of the damage a Witch could do here now.' At the mention of the word *Witch* Eric drew a sharp breath. 'It's what we've been thinking, isn't it?' she said bluntly. 'Whatever swiped that boy Paul away could have been a Witch. Let's stop pretending it hasn't crossed our minds. There was definitely something powerful with him.'

'Dragwena is dead,' said Morpeth. He came across and held her gaze. 'She can't harm you any more. And I see no evidence yet that there are other Witches here.'

Rachel nodded bleakly, wanting desperately to believe that.

'We need more information,' Morpeth said. 'Rachel, could you attune your information spells to find only those children actually *using* their magic?'

'Yes,' she said. 'I suppose that would tell us how many there are, and where. But we need to find out *how* they're using their magic as well. Are there other dog-tormentors like Paul out there? I want to get closer to them.'

'Good idea,' said Eric. 'And me and the boys'll come with you.' He shot the prapsies a special look. 'Extra protection.'

'No, I'm going to have to travel long distances,' Rachel told him. 'It's too difficult for me to do that with you hanging on.' She stared at Morpeth, seeing that he was about to object. 'I'll go on my own,' she insisted. 'It's safer that way.'

'Is it?' he asked, noticing her eyes glowing an almost painfully pure blue. 'Or is that the advice your flying spells are whispering?' Rachel hesitated, questioning herself. 'We need to be careful,' Morpeth said. 'Something attracted Paul here. What else could it be except your magic, Rachel? He probably knows where you live; and, willingly or not, he did attack you.' Morpeth glanced out of the window. 'Perhaps he's waiting for a second chance, when Eric and I aren't close enough to protect you.'

Rachel sighed heavily. 'I can't leave Mum here alone with *him* out there,' she said. 'I need you both to stay with her. Please, Morpeth. At any sign of danger I'll turn back. I promise.'

Morpeth wondered what to do. Was the boy Paul lurking patiently somewhere out there, preparing a better attack? And who was his invisible companion? A Witch, wanting Rachel dead? However, they did need to know more about this sudden use of magic – and sheer speed, unencumbered speed, was probably Rachel's best defence against an unknown opponent. Finally, he assented.

Eric shook his head. 'What do we say to Mum? She'll freak out.'

'Leave that to me,' Morpeth told him, knowing Mum would never accept his decision to let Rachel leave the house.

Rachel quickly kissed Eric, hugged Morpeth and squeezed past him. Unbolting the front door she hurried into the garden, trying not to think too much about what might be waiting for her. Outside the sky was clear and sunny.

A Witch could see me for miles, Rachel thought.

Feeling like a target standing in the porch, she quickly considered what shape to assume. Shape-changing was one of her special magical gifts. She had discovered it on Ithrea, improved it in her battles with Dragwena, and practised it repeatedly over the last couple of weeks. She didn't want to make a mistake now. What form to choose?

What would be the least conspicuous object in this wide-open sky?

A few swallows above swooped for insects. Carefully, making sure no one else was watching, Rachel transformed herself into one. Unfurling her sleek feathers, she flitted into the suddenly menacing skies.

7

the BLue-sky RAINBOW

Rachel soared into the warm summer morning air. For a moment she saw Morpeth, Eric and the prapsies glancing up through the lounge window. Then their anxious faces vanished as she used her tough swallow wings to beat a path upwards.

As familiar houses and streets dwindled the spiky-haired image of Paul swam back into her mind.

Practise your magic, she told herself, trying to shrug off the fear.

Tucking in miniature claws, Rachel deliberately threw her feathered body about the skies. Despite recent practice at home some parts of her spell-making, especially her flying spells, were still rusty. Come on, she thought, inviting her magic forward: surprise me!

Countless manoeuvring spells eagerly offered themselves. They promised wonders. Rachel selected two, tracing a wonderfully extended arc across the sky – a trick no swallow had ever attempted.

She felt nervous about remaining one shape for too long. How fast can I change if I really push hard? she wondered. She plucked out another bird-shape at random: a kestrel.

Lengthening her wings, Rachel hovered in the air, the terror of mice!

Something else, she thought. Don't stop to think.

In mid-flight, mid-flex-of-wing, she made herself alter again and again. A dove. A quick-darting hummingbird. A glorious swan, beating its ponderous wings. Rachel flew across the sky and up, up into its broad reaches, testing herself, transforming into every bird she knew.

And then a different spell suggested a *bat*.

Instantly her bird eyes shrivelled. Rachel sent out sonar clicks, and from a wrinkled, scrunched-up head she witnessed a place more beautiful than anything she had ever seen with her own or bird eyes. It was a fabulous new world, a bat world, without colour, but where each blade of grass, every tuck of air, had an exquisiteness of texture she had no words to describe.

You don't need these primitive wings to fly, her spells said. Just point your feet!

Giddy with excitement, Rachel transformed back into a girl and simply kicked her shoes through the air.

The turbulent wake of a supersonic jet caught her eye.

Catch it! Rachel commanded. A shifting spell willingly obeyed. The air lurched, flinging Rachel forward. There was no sensation of flight. Within a heartbeat, less than that, she stood on the nose-cone, peering in the cockpit. The pilot blinked in disbelief at the girl smiling at him through the window.

Rachel allowed the jet to fly on and focused on a remote cumulus cloud. How far away? she asked her information spells. 0.73 miles, they answered smoothly. Take me there! A shift took control, drawing her to the cloud – and then she shifted onto another cloud, and another, pushing herself to ever greater distances: a mile; five miles; ten; fifty. How about *eighty*!

Rachel chucked herself recklessly about the sky.

Eventually she stopped, skidding to a halt. Remember what you came out here for, she told herself angrily. Mum and the others are unsafe at home. Start searching for signs of magic ...

How could she find the most gifted children? Magic has a distinctive smell, her spells reminded her – hunt out its scent. Her own nose was hopeless. Rachel allowed the spells to take charge. They grew her nostrils until each split into a soft, fleshy flap, like fragile petals that wavered in the breeze.

She sniffed – and immediately noticed the faint aromas of children's magic.

Some of the smells were sharp and pungent, others musky, fragrant, ripe or a mixture of these things, and all the traces were weak. To find those like Paul actively using magic she needed to search a wider area and shift faster.

Rachel made herself relax, permitting the magic to flood through her veins. The feeling thrilled: it was nervy and wild, like breathing immaculately clean air after a lifetime of mustiness. She had felt flashes of the same exhilaration when she fought Dragwena on Ithrea, but fear had spoiled any pleasure she might have enjoyed then. Now she turned confidently into the wind. Closing her eyes, she forgot about clouds. She sniffed for the tiniest vestiges of magic – and launched herself at them.

In great leaps she shifted, leaving home far behind. Cities blurred past. Seas surged up to meet her and receded like dreams of seas. Her body hugged a coastline, and she touched the wet rocks where a child had recently tried his first spell. But he had gone, and Rachel shifted again. Following a striking scent she entered a different country where the air was hot and the smells new.

Her shift had carried her to southern France.

Feeling exposed, she hid as a fly, settling on the needle-leaf of an Aleppo pine tree. She was in the mountains of Provence. At this time of the year, early summer, the air was already dry and hazy. Heat shimmered from the burning Gorges de la Nesque cut into the high mountains. And barely visible amongst the elegant pines on the steep slopes Rachel found a boy. He might have been four years old, probably less.

In a flawlessly blue sky he had created a *rainbow*.

It towered above the mountains, violet and red and yellow stripes dripping like paint onto the land below. '*Plus grand, plus haut!*' he shouted, laughing at the sun.

Rachel translated as best she could with her shaky

French – 'Bigger! Higher!' – and felt elated. There's no danger here, she thought – just a boy learning to use his newly awakened magic. Changing back into a girl she approached him with outstretched arms.

'Don't be scared,' she said, as he pulled back in surprise. '*Je suis Rachel. Qui es tu?*'

The boy stared intensely at her, then cursed when he realized he had forgotten about his rainbow. He squinted up to see all the colours vanish. Stamping his feet and scowling, he ran off down the mountains, his sandals slapping the hard soil.

Rachel considered following him – but a stronger scent had already attracted her attention. She hurriedly shifted again. This time, disguised as a wasp, she came down in Dortmund, Germany.

Where a girl, so young that she still required a bulky nappy, climbed an apple tree in a garden.

The child's mother stood nearby, too shocked to move. From the tree top the baby held out her arms, calling: '*Bär! Bär!*' At first Rachel thought the little girl must want her mother – then she saw the teddy bear lying in the grass. As Rachel watched, the bear's stitched button-eyes blinked. It sprang up. On felt pads it skipped across the lawn and clambered up the tree trunk, flinging its furry arms around the girl.

Both baby and bear turned together to gaze at the mother.

Rachel shook her head, trying to make sense of it. Perhaps this wasn't so strange. If young children experimented wouldn't they start with their toys? There's nothing actually sinister taking place here, she decided. Just a child at play.

While Rachel wondered how to console the distraught mother, a new scent hit her. It was different from the others. This smell was deeply rich and vast, as if a great shoal of gifted children had come together to make it. For the first time Rachel felt truly frightened. Could this be the magic of a *single* child?

Investigate, some of her spells advised. Flee, ordered the rest.

Rachel made herself shift towards the scent. She moved swiftly, back across France, skirting Spain, travelling southwards, until she reached a new continent: Africa.

The searing heat of the Sahara Desert blazed under her. She shifted at tremendous speed over the sand dunes, and became suddenly aware that her own gifts alone could never shift her at this pace. Something else had registered her presence. It knew she was out there, and drew her to it, a colossal, restless force heaving her into its own domain.

When she reached her destination Rachel felt herself almost yanked from the sky.

She staggered, a dazed girl, too shocked for a moment to think of concealing herself.

She stood in a Nigerian village, beside a round hut. The hut was made from mud bricks mixed with straw, and in the shade of one of its walls a baby boy sat on the baked soil. He was covered in beautiful yellow butterflies. Dozens of them rested contentedly on his fingers, his bare feet, his hair. They settled like jewels on his earlobes and his eyelids. The sight of so many insects should have been grotesque, but Rachel instinctively realized they were commanded by the baby. This little boy was the source of all the astounding magic that had drawn her here.

As soon as he saw Rachel the baby smiled. It was a simple, genuinely child-like smile of welcome.

'Yemi,' he said, pointing proudly at himself. 'Yemi.'

Rachel cried out with happiness as an astonishing feeling surged through her. It came from Yemi. He could only speak a few words, yet his spells already knew a full greeting. The magic welled freely out of him, so instinctive and yearning, so grateful to find it was not alone in the world.

Without thinking about it Rachel ran across, swept Yemi up in her arms and threw him into the air.

Momentarily he hung above her head, not falling. Kicking his bare feet, he struggled to keep himself aloft. When he did fall it was the helpless way any other baby would fall. Rachel caught and held him close, whispering her name into his butterfly-thronged ears. He blew the Camberwell Beauties onto her. They fanned out, adorning her hair with their yellow loveliness.

Then a gasp from the hut made Rachel turn.

Yemi chuckled. 'Fola,' he announced.

Rachel saw a girl half-inside the hut, clinging to the door frame. Her hair was braided and daubed with flour, and she glanced fixedly at Rachel, seemingly in awe.

'Hello,' Rachel said, withdrawing the spell-colours from her eyes to avoid frightening her. 'I'm sorry if I startled you. Did you see me arrive just now?'

The girl had trouble understanding Rachel's language.

70

Finally, she nodded. 'Who are you?' she asked in heavily accented English. 'What you want with us?' She spoke mildly, and with great curiosity, glancing at Rachel's clothes and skin and hair.

Another voice, much harsher, coming from inside the house, shouted something – and Fola's collar was tugged. She resisted, clearly wanting to linger with Rachel.

'Is that your mum in there?' Rachel asked. 'Is she scared? She mustn't be. I won't harm Yemi. Please, if—'

The house voice rumbled menacingly.

'You make Mama afraid,' Fola said. 'Yes, the two of you. Have you come take Yemi away?'

'Of course not,' Rachel said. 'Are you his sister?'

'We hide him very safe,' Fola muttered. 'Yemi no suppose to be out. Mama keeps him in, then he escape.' She gazed at Rachel searchingly. 'He know you de coming, didn't he!' She was tugged again. 'Yemi, come!' Fola insisted.

She reached out an arm, but Yemi did not want to leave Rachel. He held her tightly and kicked out at his sister.

'No, do what she asks,' Rachel said. 'I'll come back. Soon.' Her magic sent waves of reassurance through to him.

After a short tantrum Yemi reluctantly slid into Fola's embrace.

'She no won you to come back,' Fola said sadly. 'Mama said that. Don't come back. Leave us alone.' But she gave Rachel a brief smile before drawing Yemi into the hut. The door was barred and a fierce argument started inside.

Rachel shifted away from the house, still tingling from the pleasure of just being with Yemi. For a while she drifted in the upper sky, thinking about him. His magic was so passionate, so joyful. Was he unique?

Before she could even begin to answer such questions another trace of magic demanded her attention. She wanted to rest, get back home and discuss what she had learned with Morpeth. However, she didn't want to ignore such a forceful scent – and this time it was familiar. She shifted.

And came down in Alexandria, Egypt.

Here, in the broad harbour where the river Nile meets the Mediterranean, there was chaos amongst the fishermen. These were tough, swarthy men used to the hazards of the sea, but nothing in their gritty lives had prepared them for this.

From the wet decks of their boats, the fish caught that day were slithering across to attack them.

8

the stone angel

Rachel saw the cause at once: on a jetty, close to the banks of the sea, stood a plump boy with spiky hair.

'Paul!' She shifted alongside him. 'What are you doing? Stop it!'

He turned despairingly towards her. 'I ca-can't! I daren't!'

Trembling, apparently fighting his own hands as they danced through the air, his fingers continued to orchestrate the biting fish.

'Get away from me!' he begged. 'I might – No! No!'

Suddenly he pulled in both arms hard. All the fish leapt from the boats – at Rachel.

She hastily created two counter-spells: one to deflect most of the fish into the water; another to rid them of the fury.

'What's happening?' Rachel demanded. 'Paul, who's making you do this?'

Before he could answer Rachel felt his body ripped away. One instant Paul was in front of her; the next he'd vanished, and as before the trail of magic was dead.

The fishermen crossed their hearts and watched Rachel from the empty boats.

A few of the fish had landed close to her. Their mouths opened and closed, and inside the soft jaws Rachel saw something she recognized: teeth; teeth that were curved, triangular and black – the teeth of a Witch.

She fell to her knees on the wooden boards of the jetty, gasping for breath.

Dragwena is dead, she told herself. You know that. She *is* dead.

But no fish on Earth had ever possessed a mouth filled with curved teeth like this. The triangularity and blackness could only mean one thing – another Witch was here.

The first three children, she realized, were using magic harmlessly enough. Paul's pattern was the same one she had seen with the Labrador – a deliberately cruel use of spells. But now she was certain Paul himself was not responsible.

Rachel could not wait to get away from the fish still flopping on the jetty. Shifting rapidly towards home, she was more than halfway back when a new scent struck her like a punch. It came from the opposite side of the world. She reeled in the sky, wanting so much to ignore it and get back, worried more than ever about leaving Morpeth, Eric and Mum without her protection. But something about this scent would not be dismissed.

Following the trail of magic Rachel streamed south-wards. She passed over the equator, deep, deep into the southern hemisphere, leaving the sun's warmth far behind.

And alighted in a Chilean graveyard.

It was night in this part of the world – and winter. Snow had recently fallen. Rachel hurriedly transformed into the first bird she associated with cold weather – a robin – hoping that she blended in. Puffing out her chest feathers, she gazed about. The graveyard was enormous. Neglected tombstones lay flat on the ground; others poked up at odd angles, as if even the dead souls beneath had tried to push their way out into a cosier place. A fullish moon squatted near the horizon. All around Rachel the scent of magic was almost unbearably concentrated. Surely not another child, she thought. It must be a Witch. A trap?

She hopped cautiously among the mossy headstones. Nothing moved in the graveyard. There were no people tending or walking between the wilderness of graves, or obvious pathways guiding the way through. Rachel ner-vously flitted between a few scattered trees. Their branches were heavy with snow that crackled under her claws. Suddenly she wished for a sign of human life – any sign at all – a voice, or even a footprint to indicate that loved ones really did visit this place. There were no such reassuring signs. The snow hugged the ground as if it had always done so, and the moon watched Rachel in the spaces between the graves. It was entirely still and frozen and silent.

Eventually Rachel found herself drawn to one remarkably beautiful statue at the centre of the graveyard.

It was a stone angel.

There were further angels dotted at intervals, but this particular angel was different. It seemed new – freshly made – and the sculpture work was so fine that the smooth lines of the face appeared virtually human. Curious, Rachel flew warily towards it.

The statue was a female angel – a girl – and it knelt exactly as a living girl might kneel on the ground. But then Rachel noticed that it had no wings. And instead of the usual prayer-like pressing of hands together, this stone girl had folded arms.

The figure looked, Rachel thought, as if it was bored.

She glanced around. There were no children here, or Witches, nothing obvious to fear; there was only a great magic, centred on the unusual statue. Rachel shook off her robin shape, moved to within a few inches of the face and reached out her hand.

'Don't touch me,' whispered the angel.

Rachel froze – and saw the stone eyelids slowly open. The rest of the girl's face remained fixed. For a moment the two girls simply gazed at one another: stone at flesh. Then Rachel felt something probing her mind. A welcome greeting, similar to that from Yemi? No, she realized. It was infinitely more sinister than that – a measuring spell, trying to judge the strength of her magic.

Rachel prevented it – and saw the girl's eyes widen.

'How did you do that?' the girl asked, trying to hide her surprise. Her voice was flat – clipped and unfriendly – and it had no fear of Rachel's magical gifts. 'Tell me how you blocked my spell,' she insisted. 'Come on, spit it out.'

'What if I refuse?'

'I'll hurt you. I mean it.' The girl watched Rachel's reaction closely.

'Hurt me?' Rachel tried to sound unconcerned. 'Why should you want to do that?'

'You might attack *me*, that's why.'

'I don't even know who you are.'

'Target practice, maybe,' the girl said, shrugging. 'Can't be too careful. You're strong, like me, I can tell. Have you tried out your spells on other children yet? You know, experimented on them?'

'Experimented?' Rachel felt her heart race.

'Oh, don't go all weak-kneed,' sighed the girl. 'Don't tell me you're squeamish when it comes to other children. What a *good* girl you must be. How disappointing.'

She dissolved her stone body and stood up, twirling in the snow as if to display herself.

Rachel could now tell that they were about the same age and height. In all other ways they were different. Pale-complexioned and angular, the girl's thin fingers and wrists jutted from her grey pullover. Her fine hair was perfectly white – almost transparent – falling lankly over her narrow shoulders. Eyebrows that were bleached, nearly hairless, shone in the moonlight. But the girl's most astonishing features were her eyes. They were a washed-out blue, lighter in colour than any Rachel had ever seen.

'I'm Heiki,' the girl said. 'What do you make of me, Rachel?'

Rachel gasped. 'How do you know my name?'

'A secret. Are you afraid?'

'Do you expect me to be afraid?'

'Of course,' said Heiki. 'The other children were afraid.'

'Did you harm them?'

'A few.' She laughed. 'Not much. Most kids are pathetic, not worth the trouble. Are you like them, Rachel? Or can you fight?'

Rachel paused. What was she to make of this girl? Her accent was odd, not English, though she spoke fluently.

'Where are you from, Heiki?'

'It doesn't matter. Haven't you even learned that yet? We don't belong anywhere any more, Rachel. Special ones like us can go where we want. And we can do what we want. Have you used your magic against any adults yet?'

'Have you?' bristled Rachel.

'That's better! Get angry!' Heiki smirked. 'You sound more interesting when you snarl. Go on. Growl a bit. Grrr. I'd prefer you meaner.'

'Have you hurt any adults?' Rachel demanded.

Heiki did not answer, but her smile widened – and Rachel, suddenly, became aware that there was a third presence with them in the graveyard. It stood alongside Heiki, watching Rachel. Rachel could not see it, but she felt its casual observation on her, and recognized the pattern at once from her time with Dragwena: a Witch. Rachel took a step backwards and tried to control her trembling. Did Heiki realize, or was she being secretly followed?

'Who told you other children are pathetic? A Witch?'

Heiki's voice faltered. 'What … do you mean?'

'I think you know very well,' Rachel said. 'A creature with four sets of black teeth and a snake.' She forced herself to look at the empty space to Heiki's right. 'They're ugly. Quite easy to spot.' She studied Heiki's guarded expression – and realized with horror that Heiki *did* recognize the description.

Heiki and the Witch were working together.

Flee! Flee! screamed Rachel's spells.

'How many Witches are there?' Rachel asked, unable to keep a quaver from her voice. She could no longer bear to look at the space next to Heiki. Jumping backwards, she shouted, 'Show yourself!'

Heiki smiled. 'What's the matter, Rachel? Scared of a few gravestones?'

'I think you'd better tell me what you know,' Rachel said, making herself step forward close enough to grasp Heiki's arm. 'Where are you from? Not this part of the world, anyway. You're a long way from home, aren't you? A long way from safety. Better tell me everything.'

'What if I won't?'

'I'll force it out of you.'

'Go on,' cried Heiki, her face excited. 'Just you try!'

Rachel launched a paralysing spell. Without harming Heiki it disabled her defences and immobilized her body, allowing only her lips and larynx to move. 'Tell me!' Rachel pressed, trying desperately to ignore the presence of the Witch.

'What are you doing?' squealed the girl, using her spells

to try to pull away. In that moment, Rachel sensed Heiki's great abilities. Fortunately, so far she could only partially control her magic.

'Tell me how many Witches there are,' Rachel said. 'And where they are.'

'You'll not force anything out of me!'

Rachel sent an information spell into the girl's ear, seeking access to her memories.

Heiki started to shake.

'What's wrong?' Rachel said, alarmed – the information spell should not have injured her.

'No! Please!' shrieked Heiki.

'I'm not—' Rachel began, then realized Heiki was not talking to her. She was communicating with the Witch.

'No, don't!' Heiki pleaded. 'Not yet! Let me fight her. I can take her on my own. I don't need your help. Let me—'

Suddenly Rachel gripped nothing. With a final groan of dismay Heiki's voice trailed off, leaving only the deserted graves. For a few minutes Rachel stood alone, feeling snow land and melt on her hot skin.

Then a new voice breathed in her ear.

'Hello,' it said. 'I am Calen.'

Rachel could see no face, but breath stirred the snowflakes above her head.

'I am the thing that frightens you most, child,' said the voice. 'Are you ready for what will happen next?'

Rachel could not move or breathe.

'Practise your magic, girl,' said the voice. 'The next time you meet Heiki she won't require my help.'

The voice faded on the breeze, but Calen left a sign – snow; not white snow but grey, falling with relish on Rachel and the tombstones of the dead.

9

GAMES
WITHOUT LIMITS

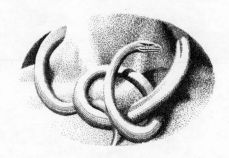

Rachel shifted frantically home from the graveyard. When she arrived in the garden Eric, Morpeth and Mum ran out to her.

'What's wrong?' cried Mum, seeing Rachel's haggard expression. 'What happened?' She clutched Rachel tightly, feeling her shiver. 'Oh, you're safe at least...'

Rachel blinked, trying to get her bearings. 'How long have I been gone?'

'Hours,' said Eric. 'What did you find? More dog-hating boys?'

'Worse than that,' she murmured.

Morpeth held her long black hair. A few grey flakes of

snow that had not melted on the journey oozed like oil against his fingers.

'Oh no,' he whispered. 'Please tell me I'm wrong.'

Rachel sagged against Mum's shoulder – and told them everything.

By the time Rachel finished Mum had long dragged them all inside the house and blacked out the windows. She sat next to Rachel in the living room, holding her in the near-darkness, and no one spoke for a while.

At last Eric said to Rachel, 'Do you think the Witch and this Heiki girl might be coming to get you, then?'

'Yes. I do.'

'Soon?'

'Probably.'

'Tonight?'

'Or earlier. I've no idea when.' Rachel gazed at the wall, her eye-colours a disenchanted grey flecked with black.

Morpeth immediately placed the prapsies on sentry duty. Seeing Eric's sombre mood, they took the task seriously, flitting between the corners of light peeping through the downstairs windows.

'Those two won't hold up a Witch,' Mum said, 'or this horrible Heiki.'

'They'll try, though,' Eric replied. 'They'll warn us fast, too, won't you, boys?'

Both prapsies waggled their heads while flying to inspect a crack in the ceiling. They stared at it with deep suspicion.

Morpeth scratched his chin. 'When Paul and Heiki were snatched away,' he asked Rachel, 'did you notice the same pattern of magic each time – Calen's?'

'Yes.' She glanced up hopefully. 'I suppose that's a good sign. Maybe Calen's the only Witch.'

'One would be enough,' said Morpeth, 'but we can't depend on there being a solitary Witch. The real question is why any Witch is here at all.' He leaned towards Rachel. 'Calen singled you out, told you her name, deliberately trying to frighten you. I'm wondering why she would do that, unless—'

'Unless she *knows* what happened to Dragwena on Ithrea,' Rachel said numbly. 'Unless Calen wants revenge.' She felt her throat tighten. 'And this strange new girl, Heiki... I bet she's being trained to fight me. Otherwise, why didn't Calen just kill me in the graveyard? It would have been easy enough.'

Mum held Rachel tightly, searching vainly for some words with which to reassure her.

'We will absolutely protect you in every way,' said Morpeth, joining Rachel on the couch. 'To help do that I'd like to know more about what Calen is attempting to do. Both Paul and Heiki appear to be under her personal instruction. Why? Are they being trained to attack you together? Or is Calen hand-picking talented children for another reason?'

'I bet this new Witch is just like Dragwena, or worse,' Eric said. With sudden passion he barked, 'Where's Larpskendya? He promised he'd be here for us. He promised!'

'I don't know,' said Rachel hollowly. 'I haven't stopped calling him. He doesn't answer.'

'Larpskendya wouldn't abandon us,' Morpeth said

firmly. 'But for now we have to find a way to survive without the Wizards. There has to be a way to fight back.' He paced the room, watched by the attentive prapsies. 'If we could eavesdrop on Calen when she interacts with children, we might understand this better. Paul is still trying to resist, we all saw that. Calen hasn't broken him, yet.'

'He might be tough,' said Eric.

'If Calen is anything like Dragwena, it doesn't matter how tough Paul is,' Morpeth replied. 'He won't be able to resist for long. We need to help him and children like him quickly.'

'Children like that aren't going to be easy to find,' said Rachel. 'The really gifted ones are scattered across the world.'

Eric laughed harshly. 'We'll find them all right. It's the end of the summer holidays tomorrow, remember. Any kids trained by Witches will hardly be able to wait!'

'For what?' asked Morpeth.

'To get inside their classrooms, of course,' Eric said. 'I bet any kids trained by Calen can't wait to use magic on their teachers!'

Before they went to bed that night Eric gave the prapsies strict instructions to stand vigil at all the windows and doors.

'They won't be able to be everywhere at the same time,' argued Rachel.

'Oh won't they?' said Eric. 'Have you forgotten how fast they were on Ithrea?' He clicked his fingers. Instantly the prapsies darted through the open doorways of the house. They moved at speed, so swiftly that Rachel knew they must be in another room a moment after leaving the last.

Eric slept uneasily on the couch. Rachel, Morpeth and Mum did not sleep. All night they huddled together on cushions in the shadows of the living room, planning and watching: watching the black windows, expecting an attack. No attack came. When dawn arrived the sun emerged cheerily as usual, as if nothing was wrong in the world.

Mum rustled up a breakfast of toast and eggs, which they ate in virtual silence. Mum was too distracted to notice the prapsies sucking tomato ketchup off Eric's plate.

'I've changed my mind,' she erupted suddenly. 'I don't care what I said last night. You're not leaving the house. None of you. I must have been mad, thinking to let you go.'

Rachel sat beside her. 'Mum, you agreed. I'll have Eric and Morpeth with me this time. We're just going to stay in the background and find out what we can. That's all.'

'But you have no idea what might be out there! I'm your mother,' she said simply, her tears flowing. 'How can I let you walk out of that door? How can I do that? I can't.'

Morpeth said to her gently, 'All the choices are difficult now, but we know a Witch is certainly out there. If we wait timidly inside these four walls Rachel and Eric are easy targets.' He saw Mum trying to formulate an objection, and said forcefully, 'Calen signalled her intentions clearly in the graveyard. On Ithrea fear prevented most children from taking any action against the Witch. Let me tell you: Dragwena took no more mercy on them for that. In fact, she despised their weakness and killed them sooner.'

Mum buried her face in Rachel's lap and Rachel silently motioned for the two of them to be left alone for a while. Morpeth and Eric went upstairs and made final preparations to depart.

'We can't take the prapsies,' Morpeth said. 'They're too noisy. We'll never shut them up.'

'Yeah, all right,' grumbled Eric. 'I know. If a cat yawns they freak out.'

He coaxed the prapsies back to his bedroom, whispering a few words of encouragement. As soon as they realized they had been locked inside, both child-birds clawed forlornly at the door.

Returning downstairs, Morpeth and Eric found Rachel still half-draped in Mum's arms. 'Let's go,' Rachel said, extricating herself with difficulty. 'Mum's agreed to let us leave if she can come with us.'

'No,' said Morpeth. 'That would be a mistake.' He faced Mum, and her stricken gaze. 'Rachel is going to have enough to concern her. If she has to protect you as well, that's an extra worry, another distraction. If Calen is anything like Dragwena, she'll probably try to hurt you just to get at Rachel.' He paused, turning to Rachel. 'That also goes for your dad. Now that we know something of Calen's purpose, he should be kept as far away as possible.'

'Too late,' Mum said. 'I called him yesterday. He's already on his way back.'

Morpeth sighed. 'I know how difficult this is,' he

implored her, 'but he mustn't come home. Tell him to go to a location not known by you, Rachel or Eric – a place never mentioned in this house.'

Mum stared furiously at Morpeth. 'If we're such a risk to Rachel, what about you? You're just an ordinary man now. Without magic, aren't you gambling with Rachel's life by accompanying her?'

Morpeth said nothing to this, and it was Rachel who spoke up.

'Mum, I need Morpeth with me. I need him.' She met her mum's intense stare. 'Morpeth took care of himself on Ithrea, and me and Eric. If you're with me, I'll just worry. All the time.'

Mum slowly nodded, and the four of them made their way through the hallway. For a while Mum stood partially barring the front door. At last her whole body seemed to cave in and she held each of them in turn and said a few words they could barely hear through her sobbing. Then she opened the door, her hands lingering on the heads of her children as they pressed past her.

'Close it, Mum,' Rachel said softly.

Mum did not close the door. She simply stayed where she was, clutching the frame as if by keeping the door open and by maintaining a gaze on her children she could keep them safe.

'I *will* protect them,' Morpeth promised, pulling it shut himself.

Rachel glanced anxiously about. Outside the house a milk float trundled up the street, followed by a stray dog. It was still too early for school children.

All three crept timidly along the path to the gate, scanning the pale cloudy sky.

'It seems safe,' said Morpeth. 'Can you detect any magic, Rachel?'

'No,' she said. 'But I don't want us standing out here like dummies. Get ready.'

Morpeth screwed his eyes painfully tight. Eric grinned.

As they had agreed the night before, Rachel turned all three into common sparrows. She had learned how to use such transforming spells on Ithrea, but it was complex and required all of her focus. She shifted them to a point high above the house. Morpeth looked uncomfortable and almost clattered straight into a tree. Eric, on the other hand, sped about with ease, as though he always went for a flight after breakfast.

'Come on,' said Rachel. 'I can't keep all three of us concealed like this for long. We need to hurry.'

She led them over the nearby streets. They skimmed close to the ground, faster than any bird, though not so fast that Rachel would miss any telltale smells of magic. Her scent flaps swayed delicately in the light winds either side of her beak.

'Phew, they're weird,' said Eric, watching the flaps quiver. He peered under his wing. 'Which school should we try first? Ours?'

'No, further out,' she said. 'There's nothing round here.'

They swooped across town, circling several infant and junior schools. The school day was now beginning, with children being called from playgrounds into assembly or first lessons. Rachel detected nothing unusual, so they searched in other towns.

Eric started trilling, a bizarre warble no sparrow had ever made.

'Stay close to me,' Rachel said. 'I've found something.'

Tracking a familiar magical signature over a hundred miles away, she shifted them towards it. Eric shut his beak as they passed over a large, four-storied junior school. Its red brick buildings appeared quiet and orderly. Dropping lower, Rachel hovered level with the third-floor windows.

Eric bumped against her wing. 'What is it?'

Within a classroom all the children sat attentively.

'I see nothing strange here,' said Morpeth.

'Check again,' Rachel told him.

Flying closer, Morpeth realized that he recognized one of the students.

'Paul!'

Morpeth narrowed his sharp bird-eyes. Paul and the rest of the class faced the teacher. The teacher herself stood stiffly, with her back to the students. On a whiteboard she had drawn a detailed head-to-foot picture of herself. In one hand she tensely held a pen; her fingers were white with the firmness of her grip. In her other hand she held an eraser, poised to use. Behind her, on the desk, the teacher had placed her shoes. Next to her shoes there were also her neatly folded pullover, several hair grips, a bracelet, earrings and a neckerchief.

Morpeth stared at the drawing the teacher had made of herself. The earrings and other items on the desk had been erased from the drawing, roughly removed.

'What's happening?' Eric breathed.

'Let's see.' Rachel used a cloaking spell to shift through the glass, and carried them to a position at the back of the classroom.

'Wrong answer again, miss,' they heard Paul saying. 'Call yourself a maths teacher? Surely you can do better than that.' He winked at a few of his friends. 'What shall we remove this time, eh?'

All the students were watching the teacher with a mixture of dread and fascination. Most were open-mouthed, uncertain what to think or do. A few of the braver ones edged away from Paul.

'Don't,' said one girl at the front of the class. 'That's enough, Paul.'

'Not yet, it isn't,' he muttered defensively. 'What's the matter with you lot, anyway? It's all just a bit of fun. I'm not going to hurt her.' He glanced at the teacher. 'Your glasses this time please, miss.'

Trembling slightly, the teacher rubbed out the glasses on the whiteboard. Then, with a flourish, she whisked off her real glasses and placed them on the desk beside the other items.

'Are you simply going to let him do this, Rach?' Eric growled. 'Don't just sit there! Do something, or I will!'

'Wait,' said Morpeth.

'Wait for what?' Eric asked angrily.

'For worse to come. Rachel, do you detect a Witch?'

She nodded grimly. 'It's Calen, keeping out of sight.'

'Stay calm, both of you,' Morpeth warned.

'Stay calm?' Eric protested. 'What's Paul doing to that teacher?'

'He's just denting her dignity a little,' said Morpeth. 'I doubt Calen will be satisfied. Keep watching.'

Paul settled back in his chair. 'Try this one, miss. Forty-seven times three hundred and fifty-five. That's not too hard.'

'I'm not … sure,' she said, still facing the board. 'Paul, please don't make me do this. I—'

'Just answer the question,' Paul told her, his voice wavering slightly.

The remaining students had fallen silent. They stared nervously at the teacher.

'It's … it's … seventeen thousand six hundred and forty-two.' She winced, realizing the answer was wrong.

Paul looked awkward. He glanced at his classmates for support, but there was none. Through their silence the teacher could be heard softly sobbing.

'Hey, all right, I get the message,' Paul said self-consciously, shrugging off the accusing glances of his classmates. 'I'll stop, then.'

The teacher's arm, still gripping the eraser, dropped to her side.

Then, swiftly, it shot back up. In a frenzy she slammed the eraser into the whiteboard and effaced her whole body.

Paul, looking frightened himself for the first time, hesitantly looked around the classroom. 'No, Calen,' he said. 'This isn't funny at all.'

An icy voice boomed, blasting in all directions

through the room. 'Really? I think it is. Continue with the game.'

Paul shook his head. 'No. I've had enough, Calen. Really, I—'

'Had enough?' laughed the voice. The glasses, shoes and other objects on the desk were thrown at the walls. 'You think *this* is enough?'

Suddenly, a thick yellow snake curled about the teacher's waist. She tried to squirm away, but her body was not under her own control.

'What are you waiting for?' Eric fumed, and Rachel also glanced uncertainly at Morpeth.

'Don't lose your nerve,' Morpeth said. 'This is only meant to frighten. The Witch wants Paul to go further. Get ready to intervene only if we must.'

Paul stared in disbelief at the snake. 'Hey, what's going on, Calen? This wasn't part of the game we agreed.'

'You stopped playing,' said the voice. 'Therefore, I changed the rules.'

The snake wriggled up the teacher's back. It slid down her neck and across her chest and knees. Touching the floor it extended its body cobra-fashion, raising its sleek yellowness fully up – and stared directly at Paul.

'Finish the game,' the snake said silkily.

'No,' Paul objected. 'You said I could do what I wanted. This is just punishment. I want to stop.'

'But *I* don't want you to stop,' said the snake. 'And this is not punishment, Paul. Real punishment is fear, taken to the furthest degree. Take the teacher to that place.' The snake moved smoothly forward until its head was inches from Paul's nose. 'Did you hear me? Or am I wasting my time with you? Perhaps I should punish you instead!'

'No, please,' Paul implored it. 'Please don't. I'll do anything you want.'

'Will you?' The snake whispered a command.

'I won't do that,' he whimpered. 'No, I can't. Don't make me.'

'You want to do it,' said the snake seductively. 'You told me that you dislike this teacher. Now *show* me how much!'

Paul retreated from the snake. It followed him to the back of the classroom, close to where Rachel, Eric and Morpeth were hiding.

'Don't waste my time,' the snake urged him. 'Just do what I ask!' Its voice became impatient. 'Why can't you enjoy this? What holds you back? You have a worthless adult at your mercy. Don't waver, Paul. You've nearly finished. One more little step. It's so easy.'

'I ... can't,' Paul said, his expression agonized. He could barely raise his head. 'It's what ... I'm not ...' He began crying, not caring what his classmates thought.

'Stop that!' raged the snake.

Paul could not hide his tears. They choked out of him.

'You useless wretch!'

A shiver passed through the snake's coils. The next moment Calen, standing over seven feet tall, disdainfully surveyed the classroom. Nylo slithered in a close yellow spiral about her neck. The children were frozen in various postures, unable to move. Calen ignored them, striding angrily around the room, kicking over empty desks and chairs. She loomed over the teacher, releasing the spells that made her face the whiteboard. Shaking uncontrollably the teacher turned. When she saw Calen, her legs collapsed. Amused, Calen waited until the teacher had heaved herself back into her chair.

'I despise you,' Calen said. 'All you have taught these children is respect for weakness.'

Unsteadily the teacher sat up. For a few seconds she simply stared in terror at the creature above her. Then, with as much assurance as she could manage, she placed the tips of her fingers on the desk to limit their shaking and gazed directly into Calen's tattooed eyes.

'Leave. Nobody wants you here.'

Calen appraised her. She walked to the whiteboard and dragged her claws, tearing the surface to shreds. 'Do you know what I could do to you?'

'I've seen enough to guess,' said the teacher. Her blouse was ruffled, her eyes still red with tears, but her voice held steady. 'Paul doesn't want to follow you. Neither will the other children here, not willingly. Whatever you are, go back to the place you came from.'

Calen punched her claw in frustration through the wall. 'I would like nothing better!' She glared angrily at Paul. 'However, first this one must learn to do *what* he is told, *when* he is told, without argument.' She swivelled back to the teacher. 'Time to teach all your precious class a new kind of lesson.'

'What are you going to do?'

'Nothing complicated,' said Calen. 'Children only understand simple threats. Get up.'

The teacher had no magic with which to fight back. She rose at once.

'Walk to the window,' ordered the Witch.

Without hesitation the teacher pushed back her chair and strode towards the glass.

'Leave her alone, Calen!' warned Paul.

'Ah, defiance,' she cried. 'At last! Stop me, then, if you can.' To the teacher she said, 'Open the window and get on the ledge.'

The teacher obeyed. Releasing the locks, she pulled the window wide, staring down at the concrete playground over sixty feet below.

'What are you waiting for?' Calen asked the teacher. She waved a claw impatiently. 'I don't want you in this class any longer.'

'No, miss!' Paul leapt forward. 'Get away from the window!' Closing his eyes, he used a spell to slam it shut.

'Good,' said Calen. 'Resist me. Is this the way I have to teach you? Drag you every step of the way? Very well. Match my spells.'

The teacher, with a strangled cry, opened the window again. She stepped through onto the narrow ledge.

'Rachel!' Eric exploded. 'What are you doing? We must help her!'

'Get ready,' Morpeth said.

The teacher bent her knees and leaned forward on her toes, ready to dive.

'Jump,' said the Witch.

'No!' screamed Paul, lunging for the teacher's legs.

He reached her in time, but the teacher, with tears in her eyes, kicked him off.

And jumped.

As the teacher fell from sight the children closed their eyes, waiting for the sound of the impact. When there was none, a few of those furthest from Calen craned their necks to look out of the window.

And their teacher looked back up at them. She was unharmed. She stood in the playground, shakily feeling her arms and legs, unable to believe they were not pulverized.

Paul numbly blinked. 'I tried … did … did I do that?'

'No,' said Calen scornfully. 'That would be too much to hope for.' She shattered the spell concealing Rachel, Eric and Morpeth.

Eric did not think. He simply ran past the desks of gasping children and jumped on Calen's back, punching her face over and over. Calen did not bother to ward off the blows. Instead she allowed Eric to repeatedly strike her slashed nose and bony eye-ridges, interested in what the punches might feel like. Finally, as if he were a mildly irritating insect, she tossed Eric aside – but gently.

Paul was dumbfounded. 'Who saved the teacher? Him?'

'Partly. The girl did the rest.' Calen's gaze slowly took in the whole of Rachel. 'You helped destroy my sister,' she said. 'It is difficult to restrain myself from killing you.'

Calen's body shook – though not with fear. Everyone in the class could see that it shook with the effort *not* to fight – to hold back on Calen's deep instinct to crush Rachel at once. Her body instinctively readied itself for combat. Blood oozed into her skin, brightening her red face. Her claws lengthened. The ligaments of her arms and legs swelled and hardened. Her eyes, the only vulnerable part of Calen's head, became slit-like, retreating inside their bony covers. And her four mouths flew wide, the black teeth aching to taste Rachel's flesh.

But she held back.

'How many of you are there?' demanded Morpeth. 'How many Witches?'

'One is too many for you,' laughed Calen. She stared at Rachel. 'There is no Wizard this time to come to your rescue, child. And while you've dallied here, your baby friend has found a new home.' She eased her broad shoulders through the window frame and vanished, taking Paul with her.

'Yemi,' Rachel whispered.

Leaving Eric and Morpeth in the classroom she shifted in great leaps to his home. Arriving breathlessly, she looked through one of the open square windows of the hut. One half of the room was in total shade. Sobbing came from the darkness, from a figure on the floor. In the sunlit part of the house sat Fola, her arm reaching into the shade to comfort the figure.

'He gone,' Fola said to Rachel. 'Taken. By this.'

Fola bared her teeth, then searched for a way to make her meaning clear. Finally she placed both her wrists against her cheeks, pointed the fingers stiffly outwards and wriggled them.

Rachel immediately sent out her information spells,

searching for the distinctive scent of Yemi, Calen or any-thing that might represent a Witch. She found nothing. Shifting rashly, she had streamed across half the world before she realized something even more sinister: Yemi's was not the only missing scent. There were no keen traces of magic left anywhere.

All the children with the strongest magic had been abducted.

10

the finest
child

From paths and roads, from the doorways of their homes, from their beds, and from every place in the world children lived, the Witches stole them. Each continent yielded its number. The Witches carried some children away directly in their muscular arms; others, those who could quickly learn rudimentary flight, flew alongside their Witch, left to wonder where they were being taken. The smallest children, when they looked at the Witch on the journey, saw only another youngster, but more wild and free-spirited than any they knew – and more persuasive. Older children were rarely treated so delicately. The Witches did not bother to hide their true appearance, and these children either kept up or were dragged in terror to the north of the planet.

Arriving at the Witch-base, they were greeted by the eye-towers. There were five, arranged in a wide circle, thrusting assuredly into the upper clouds. Each child was appointed a Witch trainer, and deposited within her tower. Here their original clothing was removed, and they were rebadged within a unisex emerald body-suit. In the youngest children it became difficult to tell boy from girl. Training began immediately in the simplest fledgling spells: flight; entrapment; concealment; basic aggression and defence tactics. Mostly the children were taught in an atmosphere of fear, but Calen had studied something of the interactions between adults and children, and for the youngest a little time was set aside for play, and enough for rest, and there were even attempts at encouragement and soft spoken commands.

The Witches were learning.

Finally Heebra herself inspected the seventy-eight children selected and prepared by her Witches.

All the children stood in lines, completely motionless. They were at attention, undergoing an endurance test in the polar snows. In midsummer above the Arctic Circle the sun never quite sets. It shines day and night, and the children had been following its arcing journey up and half down the sky for a long time. Winds cold enough to freeze human blood battered them, but they were careful not to shiver or show the slightest trace of discomfort.

'Are these the superior ones?' Heebra asked.

'Yes,' answered Calen. 'The most gifted from each country. The finest children.'

Heebra flew between the tidily arranged lines, searching for weaknesses. 'How long have they been standing?'

'Over seventeen hours.'

'Without food or rest?'

'In most cases without even moving,' Calen assured her.

'What about this one?' Heebra pointed at a dark-skinned baby boy.

'Ah, that is Yemi. At least we think so. Yemi is the main word he uses, anyway. He's the youngest of all.'

Yemi sat happily packing snow around his feet. As Heebra observed him, several large yellow butterflies perched on his toes also observed her. Their wings were the size of his face.

'He brought the insects with him from Africa,' explained Calen. 'They're growing, changing. As Yemi learns to use his magic they also develop. Yesterday they were less than half that size.'

Yemi held out his arms to be picked up by Heebra.

'What does he want?' she asked.

'It is their peculiar way of seeking attention,' said Calen, She bent down and gingerly lifted Yemi with one claw, holding him at arm's length from her jaws. All four sets of teeth strained forward to reach him.

Heebra grinned. 'You make a poor human mother.'

'His softness is appetizing,' Calen admitted, retracting her teeth.

Heebra sniffed the air, closely studying Yemi. 'There is a magnificence about him. He could be dangerous.'

'He's too young to be a threat yet,' said Calen. She showered Yemi with spiders from her jaws, dropping them between his legs. He picked them up admiringly and showed the largest spiders to his own Camberwell

Beauties. 'Our real appearance does not appal him,' said Calen. 'In fact, unlike the older children, nothing seems to frighten him.'

Heebra examined Yemi's trusting face. 'It is the intensity of our magic that fascinates him. He is drawn to it. We must keep him close, train him separately from the other children, not allow them to influence the boy. Does he miss the mother?'

'Of course.'

'Keep him near you,' said Heebra. 'Learn how to become a convincing replacement.'

'You really think he's so special?'

'I have no doubt,' said Heebra emphatically.

Yemi tickled Calen's ankle.

'Later,' she hushed him.

Heebra looked amused. 'What does he expect?'

'He wants to play a game. It is how they learn.'

'Show me.'

Calen allowed Yemi to grip a gnarled foot-claw. Holding on firmly with both hands, he squeezed his eyes tight shut with expectation as Calen took flight. After a slow climb to a few hundred feet, she kicked him off. Yemi descended inexpertly, more like a paper aeroplane lost in the winds than real flight, but he landed softly enough. As soon as he touched the ground he held up his arms for another ride.

'Yesterday he could not fly at all,' said Calen. 'Remarkable progress.'

Heebra nodded, then returned her attention to the older children.

'I take it they have all passed first-stage training?'

'Some are advanced fliers already,' said Calen. 'And, as you see, the cold is no longer a problem.'

'Yes, they're disciplined enough,' noted Heebra. 'How can we obtain their loyalty?'

'They fear us anyway,' Calen answered. 'For now we can use that to control them. Some are surprisingly unwilling to injure the adults, even when pushed.' She glared at Paul. He stood in line with the rest, shoulders slumped, his spiky hair the only mark to distinguish him from the other taller children. 'Some can be charmed,' Calen said. 'A few have had particular experiences we can exploit.' She smiled, pointing out Heiki, who gazed haughtily back. 'That girl, for instance. I have lavished particular care on her. The rest need more work, but Heiki is dependable in every way. She could pass most intermediate student challenges on Ool.'

'So confident?' said Heebra. 'Then I'll test her. And if she fails it is *you* I'll punish.'

From her own place in the lines of children Heiki tried to follow the conversation between Calen and Heebra. They appeared to be discussing her. Good. Unlike the other children, she desired to be noticed. At first she had found all the Witches' appearance repulsive; but the longer she spent with Calen the more captivated she became. Calen exuded an effortlessness of power, imposing her authority in a brash, offhand, way. And yet, Heiki saw, at the same time her gestures were lithely keen and smooth – almost graceful. And no one else seemed to notice how tenderly Calen spoke to her soul-snake, Nylo. He idolized her, wandering freely about her torso, mirroring her many moods.

From the earliest days, Calen had paid Heiki special attention. Sometimes they stood together for hours, chatting like sisters, almost as if they were equals, discussing the merits of the other boys and girls. Heiki had already learned the names of the most impressive children – Siobhan, Paul, Veena, Xiao-hong, Marshall and, of course, that oddity Yemi. She didn't care about the rest, and was still trying to decide if any of them could be trusted.

Calen parted from Heebra and glided towards her.

'Justify my faith in you,' she said huskily. 'Prove yourself the best, and your reward will be as I promised.'

'I won't fail,' Heiki said. 'Am I going to be tested? What will—'

'You'll see. Prepare yourself.'

Without warning Heiki's body was suddenly wrenched from the ground.

She stood – alone – in a large field of virgin snow near the eye-towers. At the end of the field all the Witches gradually assembled, their black dresses swept back by the wind. Most stroked polar bears – the only pets hardy enough to take the scraping of a Witch's claw. The rest of the children were bunched at the feet of the Witches responsible for their training.

'The bears will come for you,' Heebra told her. 'The test is to get past them. If you make a mistake you will not be given a second chance. Do you understand?'

Heiki nodded vigorously, afraid that if she asked any questions Heebra would interpret that as weakness. One chance, she thought. I mustn't spoil it. She shivered, and realized: I'm meant to feel frightened. That's part of the test, too.

'Most of the spells taught you by Calen are worthless here,' Heebra said. 'You cannot fly, or shift, past the bears. Find another way to cross the snow.'

As soon as Heebra finished speaking the bears picked up their shaggy hindquarters and took up positions at mathematically equal distances across the field. There were no gaps. There was no space through which Heiki might dash to the Witches. In any case she knew she could never outrun an adult polar bear.

I can do it, Heiki told herself. I'm better than the other children.

The first line of bears loped steadily towards her. Prevented from flying or shifting, Heiki tried a wounding spell on the nearest. The bear merely came on faster. She cloaked herself in a fold of wind. The bears lunged forward, still seeing her. Heiki hurriedly sorted through her other new spells. She created a replica image of her body, placing it in hundreds of places on the field; the images simply faded. The nearest bears were almost upon her now, close enough for Heiki to smell half-digested fish on their pluming breaths.

She started to panic. There had to be *something* she was allowed to do!

Glancing desperately at Calen for advice, she found the Witch's eyes were expressionless.

Then Heiki noticed Yemi. Unseen even by the Witches he had drifted across the field.

Heebra and Calen consulted. They had not expected this, but made no attempt to remove him.

Yemi meandered vaguely in the air, like a lost balloon,

and landed amongst the bears. The nearest animal lumbered towards him. Teeth bared, it lowered its great head and ... halted. Uncertainly, digging its paws hard into the snow to avoid crushing the boy, it sniffed him. Yemi raised his little hand and the bear tenderly nuzzled it.

The scent of a Witch is on him, Heiki realized – Calen's scent. Was that a coincidence? Or did he know that was the way to stay safe? Yemi pushed himself from the snow and floated serenely between the bears, heading for Calen. Sweeping all his butterflies onto his legs, he landed clumsily on her thick neck and smothered her bony red face in kisses.

Heebra's attention reverted to Heiki.

'You cannot copy Yemi's trick,' she said. 'Find a different way to us.'

The bears again turned smartly to face Heiki – but this time she was ready.

A Witch, standing near Heebra, flinched as her orange soul-snake suddenly uncoiled. It flew from her neck towards Heiki. The outraged Witch recovered immediately, but Heebra prevented her from retrieving the soul-snake.

'Wait,' Heebra ordered. 'Let's see if the child can control it.'

The snake landed in Heiki's sweating hands. Confused and angry, it wriggled in her grasp, not liking her unfamiliar touch or smell. Heiki tried wrapping the snake around her throat to calm it, in the typical style of a Witch. This only infuriated the snake more.

Intelligently, expertly, its coils began to choke her.

Heiki shrieked, trying to pull the snake from her neck – but its hold was too tenacious. If only she could use her spells!

The coils tightened a further precise notch.

Heiki was now shaking, close to losing consciousness. What to do?

What would *no* other child think of doing?

Abruptly, she relaxed. She ignored her sore throat and forced her rigid neck to untense. She flooded her mind with pleasant feelings about the touch of the snake. Baffled, the snake eased its hold slightly. Heiki continued to think the warm feelings, and gently stroked the under-side of the snake's head. She fumbled in its reptile mind and understood its soul-name: Dacon. She called that name over and over. Dacon. Dacon. Eventually she had the soul-snake's amused respect and his peach-tinted eyes met hers.

'Walk across the field,' said Dacon. 'The bears suspect you are a Witch now. They will not attack – or, if they try, I will defend you.'

Heiki walked warily across the field. The grunting bears fell back, lowering their heads. Whispering soothingly to the soul-snake all the way, Heiki walked directly up to Heebra and stood defiantly before her. Calen, close by, glowed with pride.

The Witch from whom she had stolen Dacon wrenched him back, and Heiki felt a pang – as if something precious had been torn from her.

'Do you want to hold the snake again?' Heebra asked mildly.

Heiki yearned for exactly this. It was incredibly hard not to reach out for Dacon.

'You are indeed impressive,' Heebra admitted. 'Calen did not overestimate you. Time to receive your reward.'

Heiki gazed at Heebra's heavy golden soul-snake. It exuded a magical aura so extreme that she wanted to flee – but she was determined to receive her prize.

'I want—'

'I know what you want, child.'

Heebra reached inside her dress and pulled out a thin grey snake. It was tiny, with pale ginger eyes. She arranged it decoratively around Heiki's shoulders.

'A newborn,' Heebra explained. 'See if it likes you.'

The snake contracted against her skin, finding a comfortable place.

Heiki was too overwhelmed to speak. She stayed still, so much wanting the snake to feel at ease against her sharply breathing throat.

'It belongs to you now,' Heebra told her. 'Treat it well.'

'Does that mean …' Heiki gushed, 'does that mean I've become a Witch … like Calen promised?'

Heebra laughed. 'No. Not yet, child. It is a beginning. Touch your snake. It won't bite – not you anyway. How does it feel?'

The snake welcomed her touch. Heiki passed her fingers across its eyes and the snake did not move.

'Oh, is it blind?'

'Yes. All soul-snakes start life this way,' answered Heebra. 'Use your magic. As your talent improves so will that of your snake.'

'Can I give it a name?'

'Of course. But that is not the traditional way. As your magic develops so your snake will learn to speak. Then it will *tell* you its own name. And it will also give you a true Witch name. Our snakes name us all. No human child has ever been honoured in that fashion.'

Heiki gasped. 'Oh, I want to grow fast,' she said. 'What do I need to do?'

'You need to shed blood, without caring how much.'

'I'm ready.' Heiki's eyes shone.

'No, child. I doubt that. You are ready for a minor task, perhaps.'

'I'll do anything you want.'

'Good. I want you to kill one of your own kind.'

'One of my own kind?'

'A child.'

Without hesitation Heiki said, 'Yes, I will do it.'

'Don't you want to know why?'

'If you want it killed, I'll do it,' said Heiki. 'What's the child's name?'

'There are three. The main one is—'

'Rachel!'

Heebra nodded.

'I knew it would be!' cried Heiki, clapping and dancing in the snow. 'Oh, this is a perfect day, a perfect day.'

Heebra explained what had happened on Ithrea. She also told her about the endless war against the Wizards. Heiki listened avidly. The longer the story went on the closer she felt to the Witches. They were magnificent! In fascination she drank in the detailed description Heebra gave of Ool. Heiki wanted so much to fly inside a storm-whirl, battling for her own eye-tower. Heebra warned her about Eric's unmagicking gifts, but Heiki stopped her describing Rachel's powers.

'Please don't tell me. I'll find out for myself. I don't want any advantages.'

'Good,' said Heebra. 'That is the answer a true Witch would give. Tell me how you will defeat Rachel.'

Heiki thought about what she had learned. 'Finding her is easy. I know Rachel's pattern already. I won't attack straight away. I'll get to know her first, change my appearance and scent so she doesn't recognize me from the grave-yard. I'll make her feel safe, comfy; that way she'll reveal her spells.'

'Rachel has few weaknesses,' said Heebra.

'I'll discover them. Can she heal injuries? Other people's bad injuries?'

'Yes. What are you thinking of?'

'Oh, nothing, just an idea.' Heiki noticed that the tedious endurance test was over at last, and the rest of the children had been dispersed into the usual training groups. 'Can I take some of the others with me?' she asked. 'I need them to help me deal with Eric. I'm not sure how to handle him yet... I'll think about it on the journey. It'll take us a few hours to get there, since I seem to be the only one who can shift.'

'Take anyone you like,' said Heebra. 'I am making you the leader of the children.'

Heiki smiled proudly and flew off to choose her team.

Heebra called Calen over. 'You selected Heiki well. An

independent, passionate child. It is as if she has been waiting her whole life for us to give her a purpose. Does she really believe your promise to transform her into a Witch?'

'She does,' said Calen, smiling. 'She wants to believe it so much.'

'I wish the other children were as amenable.'

'Do you trust Heiki to defeat Rachel?'

'I trust nothing,' Heebra answered dismissively. 'Rachel is too formidable to be treated lightly. Let Heiki decide her own tactics, but I want to approve them. And when Heiki leaves, you shadow her. Stay out of sight. Take Yemi with you, but keep him close – and be wary of him.'

'Wary? Of a baby?'

'He is not a typical human child.'

They both turned and watched Heiki making her selections for the team.

Heiki chose carefully, picking a mixture of those who were most talented and also those she believed would follow her orders without argument. When this had been done, she started formulating a plan, gesturing confidently, using others to translate for those children who spoke no English.

'I see there's no need for us to push them any longer,' Calen laughed. 'Young Heiki will be as exacting a taskmaster as any Witch!'

11

ambush

A small goldfish rippled the dark surface of the pond.

'Did you hear that!' screeched one prapsy, shivering with excitement.

'Shush,' the other cried. 'You'll wake Eric, boys.'

'But did you hear it?'

'I heard it!'

Like blurs, they sped together from the bathroom to the bedroom overlooking the night garden. Perched cheek-to-cheek they scrutinized the pond.

'There!' one cried wildly. 'An underwater devil!'

'A midget devil. Shall we tell Eric?'

'Don't be stupid, you mutant spanker!'

'You're stupid! Shush! Wait.'

'What?'

'Shadows.'

They both sensed the magic approaching the house.

'What is it? I'm scared.'

'Can't see it. Can't see *them*. Must be backside of house. Let's look.'

'After you,' said its companion, bowing gracefully.

'No. *After you*,' said the other – and they both flew off together.

From the living room they peered anxiously over the front street.

'See how they are creepily hiding?'

'They are scared of us!'

The prapsies' big eyes blinked violently. One licked the living-room window, wiping off the condensation; the other pressed a round face against the cleared glass. Together they twitched and gazed out over the empty street.

'What kind of things are they?'

'They are flying. Must be birds. Naughty birds, maybe. Should be in bed by now.'

'Big mad naughty birds!' A nervous giggle.

'Shall we chat to them?'

'Shut up and listen!'

'They are sneaking up, do you see?'

'I see them!'

The prapsies flapped their wings, trying to frighten off the dark shadows.

Outside nine large silhouettes emerged stealthily from the night sky. For a moment they gathered in front of the gibbous moon. Then they plunged towards the house.

'Eric! Eric!' shrieked the prapsies, fleeing upstairs. 'Rachel!'

Rachel's eyes flicked wide. Beneath her she heard glass being smashed – something invading the house. Two shattered windows, her information spells told her rapidly. One in the living room; another in the kitchen. What else? She heard frame wood hit the carpet – followed by the soft thud of shoes.

Eric blinked from a bed that had been placed close to hers.

'What's going on?'

'Stay quiet,' Rachel told him. She tried to decide who had broken in. Witches were large-bodied and heavy. These landings had been lighter.

'I think it's kids,' she said.

The prapsies were nutting the door of the bedroom. Eric let them in, pushing their quivering heads under the quilt.

'Morpeth and Mum are down there on guard!' he reminded Rachel. 'Come on!'

'Wait!' Rachel grabbed his arm.

'Get off! I'm going!'

She tugged him back. 'Listen, will you!'

Four more bodies had flown into the house. Rachel heard them squeeze through the gaping holes and land. Neat landings, Rachel thought. Both feet precisely together. Children using magic – and already experienced flyers.

'It's an ambush,' she said. 'Keep quiet. They might not know we're here.'

'What about Morpeth and Mum?' Eric fumed. 'I can't hear them!'

Downstairs glass tinkled underfoot. Even Eric's ears could now easily hear the sound of many pairs of feet tramping noisily around the living room. From his bed the prapsies kissed each other for comfort.

'Whoever they are, they're not trying to catch us by surprise,' said Eric. He lunged for the stairway. 'Morpeth! Where are you?'

Morpeth's gruff voice called up, 'I'm all right! So is your mum. Come to the kitchen.'

Eric tucked his quilt gently around the necks of the prapsies, calming them.

'Sleep, sleep, boys,' he said. 'Close your peepers.' The prapsies squeezed their eyes shut and pretended to nap because they knew that was what he wanted.

Eric and Rachel hurried downstairs.

They found Mum and Morpeth unharmed, standing by the dining table. Behind them a spiky-haired boy stood gazing out of the broken windows.

'Paul!' said a shocked Eric.

Eight more children were also crowded into the room. The curtains had been drawn back. All stared at the blazing broad moon, watching intently, as if unable to take their eyes from the sky.

Paul turned to Rachel and his eyes brimmed with tears.

'Oh, it is you, it *is*,' he murmured. 'I never thought we'd find you. You've no idea what we've been through to make it here.'

Eric glared at him. 'Where's your ugly Witch, Calen?'

She's …' – Paul choked on the words – 'given up on me. Oh, I don't mind, don't think *I* mind,' he said, but his face sagged awkwardly. 'Not good enough, you see. Wasn't *ruthless* enough.' He spread his arms, indicating those around him. 'None of us were.'

Rachel saw how distressed all the children looked. Heiki was not with them.

'How many Witches are there?' she asked. One, she thought, please just one.

'Five,' Paul answered.

Rachel tried to stay calm. Morpeth seemed unfazed by the news, and she gripped his hand.

'Why do you keep checking the windows?' he asked.

'We're being chased.'

'By Witches?'

Paul laughed bitterly. 'You think Witches can be bothered with the likes of us? We're the *rejects*.'

'Then who's chasing after you?'

'Kids, of course. Better kids. The *favourites*.'

Mum gasped. 'Why?'

'You've no idea what's going on, have you?' said Paul. 'The Witches make us fight, to see who's the best. They weed out those not up to scratch.' He glanced at his companions. A few dropped their heads. 'We lost too many battles. They've made us target practice.'

Eric asked, 'Target practice for whom?'

'For the favourites. They've caught us once. Banged us about a bit, then gave us a head start. Next time they'll finish us off. We can't outrun them. Most are quicker fliers than us. Hey, we haven't got much time, They're—'

'They're here,' a girl whispered. She staggered back from the window.

Outside a new group of children hung in a line against the rooftops. They made no attempt to conceal themselves. Kneeling or sitting at ease in the air, they all stared boldly at Rachel.

Morpeth studied Paul closely. 'How did you find us?'

'All the kids know this address,' Paul said. 'And the scent of Rachel's magic is hardly difficult to find.' He glanced at her. 'You've left trails everywhere.' From the darkness outside a child called his name, and he shrank away from the window. 'Look, are you going to help us, or not!'

Morpeth noticed that Paul and the other children's injuries were not serious – a few bruises and superficial cuts. 'I see no evidence you've been involved in a real fight,' he said.

'That's because Ciara drew them off!' bellowed Paul.

'I'm listening,' said Morpeth evenly.

'Ciara's a girl who's good enough to fight with the best kids, but she won't. She helped us get a good head start. The Witches went after her for that. They've probably killed her already.'

'We should get everyone away from these windows,' Mum said.

'No,' Morpeth replied firmly. 'We can defend ourselves better if we keep them all in sight. Those inside and outside the house.'

Mum looked curiously at Morpeth. 'Don't you believe this boy's story? Isn't Paul the one who's been resisting Calen?'

'I'm not sure what to believe yet,' Morpeth said. He turned to Rachel. 'Send out your information spells. If

Witches are attacking or have recently attacked anyone there should be some clear evidence.'

Rachel did so, and distantly sensed powerful spells being used. Some were from a child, a child raising all its defensive spells against massive forces.

'Two Witches,' Rachel breathed. 'Two Witches against one child. They're fighting now. She won't stand a chance.'

'How far away?' Eric asked.

'Hundreds of miles.'

Eric thumped the table. 'If I could get close, I could destroy the spells.' He gazed at Rachel. 'Can *you* get there in time to help her?'

'I'm needed here. I can't leave you!'

'Please,' pleaded one of the girls. 'You mustn't leave Ciara to fight on her own!'

Far off Rachel could sense Ciara's pain. She was torn: leave a poor, unknown girl to fight alone, or leave Mum with only Eric and Morpeth to defend her against the magic of the *favourites*.

'Morpeth,' she said bluntly. 'Tell me: what should I do?'

'Go,' he told her. 'Ciara can't survive long. We *can* defend this house for a while, I'm certain. Trust me: if there are five Witches out there who want us dead, even with you here we won't be able to stop them. Get to that girl, before it's too late.'

Rachel glanced at Mum who half-nodded, half-shook her terrified face.

'Wait!' Morpeth whispered in Rachel's ear. 'Can you put a scent-tag on me? A trace you could follow?'

'Yes,' she said.

'Do it.'

Rachel quickly completed the spell, and made the scent-tag difficult to detect.

Then, a long way off, she felt a child's defences suddenly shatter.

With a final agonized glance at everyone, she shifted.

As soon as Rachel left Paul buried his face in his hands.

'I'm so sorry,' he said. 'So sorry.'

'Pretty nicely done,' said another, older, pale-skinned boy, slapping Paul's back. So far this boy had been silent throughout. 'Heiki reckoned you would be the best to convince them,' he said. 'She was right. I thought you'd mess it up, actually.'

Paul half-raised his head. 'Marshall, no one here gets hurt. That's what we agreed.'

'Whatever,' said Marshall, dismissively.

He waved to the children outside. At this signal they swarmed towards the house, some calling out the names of friends inside.

'How could you do that?' Eric raged at Paul. 'How could you!'

Tears poured down Paul's face. 'I couldn't ... I—'

'Oh, shut up,' said Marshall, brushing him aside.

Morpeth drew Eric and Mum close, furiously trying to decide how he could protect them.

'I suppose that Witch Calen is with you,' Eric snarled at Marshall. 'You don't have the guts to be doing this on your own.'

'We don't need her help with Rachel out of the way,' Marshall said.

Eric raised his hands. 'Do you think I'm just going to let you do what you want? I'll snuff out all your spells.'

'Will you, now.' Two children, strength boosted by their magic, grasped Mum's arms and legs. 'We've been taught all about your weird gift,' Marshall said to Eric. 'So this is what's going to happen. You and Morpeth come with us. Mum stays here. If you interfere with any of our spells we have orders to kill Morpeth on the journey. And just in case either of you try anything funny we're leaving some kids behind to take care of Mumsy.'

'Don't you dare harm her!' raged Eric.

'We'll do what we want.'

'Your performance isn't very polished,' Morpeth said, gazing levelly at Marshall. 'You're under orders, aren't you? Whose orders? What have you been told to do with Eric's mother?'

'What do you care?' Marshall said. 'Heiki doesn't mind much what happens to her, or you for that matter. It's Eric she's got special plans for.'

Paul glanced up. 'Their mum wasn't part of the deal. And what are these plans for Eric? I don't remember anything about them.'

'Heiki didn't trust you with everything,' Marshall said.

'Marshall,' Mum tried, her eyes pleading with him. 'Look, I know … you're not impressed by me … adults generally. I suppose without magic we just seem—'

'A hindrance,' finished Marshall. 'That's right. Parents are worthless now.'

'Says who?' asked Eric angrily.

'Heiki.'

'Who's that? A Witch?'

'A girl. You'll find out.'

'It sounds like she scares *you!*' Eric said scornfully.

'Maybe she does,' Marshall muttered.

Behind them, came two panted breaths.

A girl stooped to look. 'Hey, what are these?'

The prapsies shivered in the doorway. They had crept from Eric's bed and had been fearfully watching, ready to fly at anyone who tried to touch him.

'We are biters!' one cried, opening its gummy, toothless mouth.

'Oh, they talk,' the girl gasped. 'I want one!'

There was a flurry as many of the children reached out, but the prapsies were too fast – and dodged away.

'Leave them alone!' Eric blasted at Marshall. 'Fight *me*, you coward. Or are you scared?'

'I'm not scared of you,' growled Marshall.

'You *are*,' Morpeth said, in a voice he made sure all the children would hear. 'All this brave talk. There's nothing behind it except fear of the Witches and what they'll do. Are you on trial yourself, Marshall?' He saw Marshall's eyes widen slightly. 'This task is a test you've been set, isn't it?' Morpeth said. 'Your behaviour … is being *watched*.'

Marshall glanced nervously out of one of the windows, then regained his composure. He sniffed the air surrounding Morpeth.

'No magic,' he said sarcastically. 'And I hear you're an old man in a boy's body. That's a curious thing.'

'Perhaps,' replied Morpeth. 'But I am what I am. What are you, Marshall?'

Marshall shrugged. At a signal from him the two children holding Mum gripped her tightly, while the remainder started to pull Eric and Morpeth towards the broken windows.

Eric peered at the street chimneys. 'Where are you taking us?'

'On a nice trip,' Marshall said, as if he was announcing the start of a picnic.

'Where?'

'You don't want to hear. A long, cold journey.'

'Then you'd better clothe us better than this,' Morpeth said, indicating Eric's pyjamas and his own lightweight clothes. Without waiting for an answer from Marshall, he strode into the spare room. Mum joined him, her hands shaking as she helped to look for trousers and shoes. She found a coat that fitted Morpeth, and pushed past a few children to go upstairs to get one thick enough for Eric.

'You've had enough time,' Marshall said to her, when she returned empty-handed.

'But I can't find anything!' she shouted. 'How dare… no, look, let me check under the stairs, please… I think…'

'Just get on with it,' Marshall hissed.

Morpeth took his time getting dressed, all the while looking steadily at Marshall. 'You weren't told what to do if you got any opposition, were you? What was the instruction from your Witch or Heiki? – just do away with me or Mum if we got difficult? Well, go on, then. Are you going to kill us for putting on a few clothes?'

Marshall said nothing, and Mum, discovering Dad's duffel coat at last, flung it around Eric's shoulders. She fumblingly pulled some of her own gloves – the only ones she could find – over his fingers, trying to find a reassuring smile.

'Let's go!' Marshall blasted finally. 'Come on!'

'Not yet,' Morpeth said. 'These clothes won't be enough if we're flying far. We'll need magic to keep us warm as well.'

'You'll get no special protection from me,' sneered Marshall. 'I've listened to you for long enough.' He gazed at the other children. 'You know what Heiki and the Witches will do to us if we fail,' he said. 'Get them to the windows!' The galvanized children dragged Eric and Morpeth across the room, while the two with Mum struggled to hold her back.

Morpeth caught her terrified gaze. This time he felt that he could make no promises. 'I won't let them harm Eric,' he said anyway. 'Trust that.'

The children finished hauling Eric and Morpeth to the window. At Marshall's signal they flew up the walls of the house and over the peaked roof, into the chilly night air. The prapsies followed a short way behind. They wanted to stay near Eric, but the children swiped at them whenever they hovered too close, so they stayed as near as they dared, shouting insults at the children holding his arms and legs.

While Eric could still be heard by Mum he craned his neck, calling hoarsely, 'Wait for Rachel! She'll be back soon.'

Marshall swept alongside him. 'I don't think so,' he said. 'Heiki has her now.'

Rachel arrived breathlessly over a dense oak wood.

Sensing the two departing Witches, she swooped down, searching in the undergrowth. Was she too late?

A girl lay on her face, draped across the roots of a tree. Her hair was ginger, curly, and smeared with blood – yet somehow she was alive. Rachel knelt beside her. Drawing on her healing spells she knitted the skin on the girl's back where it had been slashed by the Witches. She set the femur of her broken leg. She lowered the swelling where a claw had fastened about the girl's throat. Any doubts Rachel had about being lured into a trap were removed by the piteous state of her injuries.

Eventually the girl sat up. She swayed, seemingly dazed.

'You're safe,' Rachel said softly. 'Don't be afraid, Ciara.'

'Where have the Witches gone?'

'I'm not sure, but they're not close. I can't sense their presence.' She smiled. 'I'm Rachel.'

'We've heard all about you. The child who defeated a Witch! Wow!'

'I had help,' Rachel said distractedly. Her information spells scanned for any approaching danger. 'Why didn't the Witches finish you off? They had time.'

'Who knows?' the girl said. Her eyes glinted. 'Did you know the Witches are training a bad girl to get you? I've met her. Scary thing. Bite your head off.'

Rachel nodded. 'Where have the Witches been keeping the children all this time?'

'Mostly at the equator. That's where they train them.'

The equator? An odd choice, Rachel thought. And she wondered about this strange girl. She had not asked about Paul or the reject kids once. Was she in shock from the Witches' attack? Possibly, though she also appeared so composed. That was it, Rachel realized. This girl looked *poised*, as if ready for anything.

'We must get back to my house,' Rachel said urgently, explaining what had happened. 'Can you fly?'

'Of course.' The girl rose stiffly. 'I'm your greatest admirer, by the way. You'll murder that Heiki girl!'

Rachel sent her information spells after the scent-tag she had left on Morpeth. For some reason he had moved away from the house. 'Something's wrong,' she said. 'Let's hurry.'

'On the way I will teach you all my spells,' the girl said eagerly. 'And you?'

'We'll see.'

The girl clapped her hands in delight. 'Two friends! That's what we are!'

Rachel flew rapidly towards home. The girl matched her speed.

'You're very good,' Rachel complimented.

'I'm hopeless. Can't do shape-shifting like you, or anything.' As Rachel prepared to shift, the girl screamed. 'Sorry, that hurts so much. Please don't.'

'But we have to get back. It'll take over an hour if we can only fly!'

'No please,' begged the girl, sagging into her arms. 'Hold me! I'm still feeling so weak.'

Rachel embraced her tightly and flew as fast as she could, waiting for the girl to recover.

Heiki smiled to herself. Perhaps this was going to be *too* simple. Rachel was impressive, but easily fooled, like all the others. Far too trusting. Of course, she had gone to great lengths to be absolutely sure to convince her. Relying on Rachel's ability to heal injuries, she had allowed the Witches to really damage her badly before they left.

That's the difference between me and you, Rachel, thought Heiki. I'll go through any amount of pain to get what I want. How much pain can you endure?

'Please go more slowly,' she implored Rachel in a feeble voice, as they sliced through scattered, wispy cloud. 'I'm so very frightened.'

12

OCEAN

Morpeth counted a troupe of twenty-seven children.

Ten carried him and Eric by the arms and legs, keeping them separated. The rest formed a guarding ring. Marshall was up front, the obvious leader. Paul flew alongside him, occasionally glancing apprehensively back to Eric. There was no sign of a Witch – and no sign of Rachel.

For a while they travelled eastwards, soaring over crop-laden fields, lit by stars and the waning moon. Then Marshall turned the troupe towards the Arctic. Leaving land behind, they headed off over the churning waves of the North Sea. Intensely cold, blustery air now carved into the children. The troupe had magic to ward off the severe winds, but Eric's and Morpeth's only protection were jumpers, gloves and coats. Morpeth knew from Ithrea how to keep his limbs moving constantly to ward off frostbite, but Eric had no such knowledge. Against the raw wind Dad's big heavy coat wasn't enough. Within minutes Morpeth sensed Eric starting to fade. Was this the fate Heiki had planned for Eric, he wondered – to kill him slowly during the flight?

Not while I live, thought Morpeth.

'Eric needs more protection!' he roared over the winds.

Marshall heard him, but said nothing.

'I expect Heiki wants her cargo delivered alive,' Morpeth called out. 'If you botch it, Marshall, if we die of exposure on the journey, she won't be happy.'

'I'll insulate them,' he heard Paul say to Marshall. 'Leave it to me.'

Marshall wavered, then said angrily, 'The minimum of warmth for Eric. Just enough to make sure he doesn't freeze. As for Morpeth, he gets nothing. Do you hear? Nothing.'

Paul extended a thin warm blanket of air around Eric's face and neck. His gaze lingered on Morpeth, but he was clearly too nervous to ignore Marshall's warning.

Left utterly exposed, Morpeth gritted his teeth and bore the pain as best he could. He flexed and unflexed his fingers, trying to hold the image of Rachel in his mind while he turned his attention to the children carrying him. They were uneasy. It was obvious to him that Heiki and the Witches must have presented this task as some sort of brazen game or adventure. Most were not fooled. Morpeth spoke to them. As they flew higher into ever colder air he asked the children questions about families and friends, to remind them what they had left behind. They did not answer, clearly under orders, but their grip loosened, and their bodies moved slightly closer to guard him from the howling winds. Soon they were bending low to hear his rough voice.

Paul's layer of warmth kept Eric alive, but his body was still pierced by the cutting gusts. As time went by he fell in and out of consciousness. The prapsies stayed close, trying to convince themselves that Eric was well, tears freezing against their cheeks.

'Wake up, you precious wonder!'

'Oh wake, will you!'

'I'm scared, boys. Eric is ill.'

'No, he is sleeping.'

'Is he? Is he just sleeping?'

They kept trying to wrap their wings around Eric's exposed cheeks, but the children transporting Eric always attempted to grab them. The prapsies could never get close enough to touch him.

At one point Eric briefly awakened.

'Go away, boys!' he rasped. 'You can fly faster than these kids. Hide. They won't find you.'

The prapsies shook stubborn heads, and continued to wilfully follow, blinking and twitching and flying into the wind, trying to use their own bodies to buffer Eric from the worst of it.

Most of the time Morpeth and Eric were kept too far apart to speak. Once the groups holding them drifted close enough to exchange a few brief words.

'Where are they taking us?' Eric managed to whisper.

'I don't know.'

'Where's Rachel?'

'Not far behind, I'm sure. She will come. Stay alert, and keep moving your hands.'

Eric looked up fiercely. 'Morpeth, don't let them hurt the prapsies! Promise me!'

'I …' Morpeth couldn't find any words. He knew that if these children wanted to harm the prapsies, he couldn't prevent them.

At a growled order from Marshall the groups split apart again. For another hour they flew purposefully northwards. Morpeth began to feel desperately tired, wanting so much to sleep. He understood what that meant – on Ithrea he had seen thousands of children succumb to a last blissful drowsiness shortly before they froze to death in the snow.

He sensed the pity of those children carrying him. They obviously wanted to help, but were afraid. Afraid of who? Not Marshall. Morpeth had seen him looking increasingly troubled at the head of the troupe. Someone else. Morpeth glanced at the roof of the sky, but saw nothing.

At some point he heard Paul wail, 'Let's at least take them lower, into calmer air!' The children holding him all raised their voices in agreement, but there was only a stony silence from Marshall.

Gradually Morpeth's strength faded. His face sank lower and lower, until his eyes were fixed only on the silver and black waves. Without bringing warmth, dawn broke at last, tingeing the surf pink. For a while, Morpeth had no idea how long, the children descended. Then he smelt the tang of salt, and heard the bleak, persistent call of gulls. A blinding whiteness cut across his eyes.

They had crossed land.

Ahead, a gigantic continent of snow stretched as far as he could see.

Where were they? Greenland? The Arctic? Morpeth urged his stiff neck muscles to move. Glancing across, he saw the group of children carrying Eric drop him onto the thick snow. Eric lay on his face, without moving. The prapsies, themselves shivering with cold, landed on his head, nipping his ears with their gums, trying to wake him. Moments later Morpeth himself was softly deposited nearby. He dragged his legs across the snow and felt for Eric's pulse. There was a heartbeat – just. Severe frostbite had set about Eric's lips and hands – Mum's gloves had not been enough. Morpeth held Eric's face away from the snow and peeled off the gloves, rubbing the finger joints and tendons.

'Wake up!' he bellowed, striking Eric hard. 'You must wake up!'

The prapsies winged about Eric's head, entreating Morpeth to hurry.

'Eric has slept long enough!'

'He is colder than bones!'

All the children who had been transporting Eric and Morpeth ascended to a point high in the sky. They hung there, solemnly observing, while the relentless Arctic winds thrashed their faces. Finally an argument broke out between Marshall, Paul and the children who had carried Morpeth.

'Come down and see us!' Morpeth shouted up, still struggling to wake Eric. 'Come and see what you've done! Or are you afraid, Marshall?'

'I'm not afraid.'

Hesitantly, Marshall descended with Paul to land. When Marshall saw Eric's blistered skin, split lips and swollen, misshapen fingers, he turned away.

'It's not so easy to allow someone to die, is it?' said Morpeth. 'It takes a long time for a Witch to convince a child it enjoys that.'

Paul could not bear the sight of Eric. He stepped forward to help him.

'Don't touch, you idiot!' cried Marshall. 'You'll get us all in trouble.'

'We can't just leave him this way. Look at his fingers!'

'We're not allowed to help him.'

'You control the troupe,' Morpeth said to Marshall. 'What's stopping you?'

Marshall glanced nervously upward. 'Are you blind? I'm not in charge here.'

Morpeth followed his gaze and sensed what must be hidden in the sky: a Witch, too far away to see, but nevertheless there, watching the behaviour of each child. Fear, Morpeth thought, knowing from long experience what the mere presence of a Witch could make children do. Suddenly he thought of his old friends, and wondered if the Witches had also discovered Ithrea. No: he could not bear to consider that...

'Only the strongest will survive,' Paul said remotely. 'That's what Calen said.'

'What have you been told to do?' Morpeth asked Marshall. 'Leave us here to die?'

'No. Bring you both to the pole, if you can survive the

journey. That's what Heiki wants. She didn't particularly care if you made it or not.'

Morpeth leant close to him, and whispered, 'Is that what *you* want, Marshall? I expect you're hoping the Witch who trained you will be satisfied with just our two little deaths. Let me tell you: she won't be. This is just the beginning. She will make you kill again and again. She won't leave you in peace. There will *never* be enough deaths to satisfy her.'

Above them a girl shouted down, 'Hey, what's going on?'

'I've got to go,' Marshall said. 'I can't be seen talking to you.'

'Give me time to revive Eric!' demanded Morpeth.

'Too dangerous.' Marshall's eyes flitted upward. 'He'll have to travel as he is.'

'Eric is just like you,' Morpeth beseeched him. 'Scared, trying to survive. Are you just going to let him die on the wind?'

Without answering Marshall kicked his feet from the snow, pulling Paul with him towards the other children.

'You *can* fight back,' Morpeth cried up to them. 'Look at each other! Can't you sense your own strength?'

If they heard neither boy replied, and Morpeth turned his attention back to Eric. He tried carving a hole to get them out of the wind, but after a few inches the snow was too compacted to dig through. So instead he took off his own coat, wrapped it around Eric and brought their bodies together for warmth.

Finally Eric half-opened his eyes. The prapsies squealed

with joy, cooing like doves in his ears. Morpeth wiped the frost off his lips.

'Only the strongest survive,' Eric mumbled. 'Isn't that what Paul said?'

'We're the strongest,' Morpeth told him.

Eric had lost all sensation in his toes. For some reason this frightened him more than anything else that had happened. 'T-talk to me, old man.'

'I'm here,' Morpeth said. 'I won't leave you.'

'Where are the prapsies?'

'Breathing on your hands.'

Managing to sit up, Eric gazed affectionately at the child-birds. 'I c-couldn't feel you, boys.' He coughed. 'Hey, I don't feel so good.'

'It's all right,' Morpeth reassured him. 'Rachel will be here soon.'

Eric nodded, trying to believe it, and peered at the glistening green uniforms of the children. 'What are they w-waiting up there for? Why don't they just finish us off?'

'Because they don't want to,' Morpeth said earnestly. 'They want to stop.'

The quarrel above had gradually spread to the entire troupe, with Paul and the children who had listened to Morpeth arguing most passionately. When it ended all the children gazed down and Eric and Morpeth discerned a spell at work.

All the winds about them ceased, a warming breeze replaced the slicing wind.

'No!' screamed an enraged voice – and from her hidden location Calen streaked across the sky. She aimed straight for the troupe, her claws extended, and initially Morpeth thought she intended to tear them to pieces. But she restrained herself, and instead flew over each child, flinging out her scorn, promising punishments – and giving new orders.

Yet again the icy winds tore at Eric and Morpeth.

'We're not done yet, old man,' Eric rasped. 'I'm not waiting for Rachel.' He held out his puffed-up fingers. 'I've still got these. If the kids back home have done anything to Mum, they've done it already. I'm not just going to lie here till they decide to finish us off. Help me up.'

Morpeth hauled Eric into a seated position. Eric raised his numb hands.

'Come on,' he coaxed, blowing on the tips. 'Don't let me down now.'

Above, Calen hissed instructions to four children. Separating from the troupe, they sank fast down the sky.

Eric pointed his fingers – and the four fell helplessly. Lying in the snow, they called for the others, their flying skills gone.

'Ignore them!' Calen said. At another of her commands, half the troupe swooped down. This time they came from several directions at once, front and behind, zigzagging evasively.

Eric knocked two more from the air.

'Quick!' he barked. 'Turn me round!'

But before Morpeth could swivel him, the rest of the attackers were on them. Morpeth sank his knuckles into the nose of the first, but the rest hit hard, sending Eric and Morpeth sprawling across the snow. Breaking off, the troupe members flew to higher regions where Eric's powers could not reach.

Eric and Morpeth regrouped, sitting back to back, while the prapsies recklessly flung themselves between Eric and the troupe, hurling abuse.

'What now?' asked Eric, squinting up.

Stung by another order from Calen the troupe had drawn together. They were massed against the sun, and Eric could hear a few of the children weeping.

'They're going to come after us in one go,' Eric realized. 'All together. Wait. What's that?'

It was Yemi.

From the cloud that had concealed Calen, he floated serenely towards the children. He was surrounded by his devoted butterflies. They were now enormous, the size of cats.

'Go back!' Calen shouted. 'Go back!'

Yemi faltered, then came on, drawn by the frightened noises within the troupe. His Camberwell Beauties surged forwards like a flock of immense slow yellow birds. They mingled with the children, touching those with tear-stained faces as if trying in some instinctive way to offer comfort. Unnerving and baffling, the butterflies milled in the sky, so big and so many that the troupe was virtually lost under their beating wings.

Finally Calen fought a path through to Yemi and yanked him away. The butterflies followed him reluctantly, their antennae bowed.

'That must be the baby Rachel mentioned,' marvelled Eric. 'Did you sense his power?'

Morpeth nodded, watching in awe as Yemi twisted uncomfortably in Calen's claws, unhappy about being carried away.

Once Calen had Yemi under control, she turned back to shriek at the children. This time they were too terrified to argue. The entire troupe clustered into the tightly knit shape of a fist. Together they dropped down, heading directly for Eric and Morpeth.

Eric closed his eyes. 'What do we do now?'

'Survive,' said Morpeth, preparing to take the first blows.

The children descended on them like hail.

13

Battle

Rachel returned home with Heiki sagging in her arms.

On the way back Heiki deliberately slowed her down. Whenever Rachel tried to shift, she faked pain. Every time Rachel tried to fly fast she wept deliriously, pretending that the shock of the Witches' attack had unhinged her mind. Rachel responded by holding her close, and flying gently, gently on the night winds.

During the journey Heiki shared some spells – nothing useful, just enough to gain Rachel's trust. Rachel warily joined in, but Heiki could tell she was not revealing her most subtle weapons or defences. Fine, she thought, not wanting too easy a contest. She made certain the voyage back lasted long enough for the troupe with Morpeth and Eric to get safely away. The last few miles were difficult –

Heiki could barely wait to see Rachel's reaction to the surprise she had prepared.

A cool dawn wind blew through the broken windows of the house.

Mum was inside, talking with the boy and girl who had been left behind.

'What are you doing?' Heiki shouted at them. 'What about the punishments? You were supposed to perform them as soon as Eric and Morpeth left!'

'They changed their minds,' said Mum thickly. Drawing the children close, she hurried across to Rachel, always keeping her gaze firmly on Heiki. The boy and girl shivered, trying to hide behind Mum's back.

'This is obviously Heiki,' Mum said hastily. 'I've been hearing all about her nastiness. Be careful, Rachel.'

Heiki grinned – and the curly ginger hair, freckles and endless weeping vanished, replaced by the washed-out blue eyes.

'The girl from the graveyard,' gasped Rachel. She turned to Mum. 'Where are—'

'Don't take your eyes off her!' Mum warned. 'Morpeth and Eric were taken. These poor kids' – she clenched the boy and girl – 'don't know where, but *that one* does.' She glared at Heiki. 'She planned it all.'

Rachel thundered at Heiki, 'If you've harmed them …'

'I *have* harmed them!'

Rachel sniffed the air. The scent-tag she had planted on Morpeth led from the kitchen, ending abruptly just above the house. 'Tell me where they've been taken!'

'Do you think I'm just going to *give* you that

information?' Heiki said scornfully. 'You'll have to fight me for it. Come on: a battle. Only us two girls. The finest children. No Witches, I promise.'

Rachel scanned the area. There were no Witches; Heiki was telling the truth about that. It showed how certain she was of success. She studied Heiki's fierce, Witch-trained eyes and felt afraid.

'Stop playing games,' Rachel said. 'I can't believe you want any of this. The Witches are making you behave this way.'

'That's not true,' Heiki replied. 'The Witches want you dead, but I couldn't wait to fight you anyway.'

'Why?' Rachel stared in disbelief. 'What have I ever done to you?'

'Nothing. I've just got to know which of us is the best.'

When Rachel looked confused, Heiki shook her head and said, 'You'd better catch up, girl. The future's a magic world. Forget grown-ups. Mums and teachers and grannies don't matter any more. Calen told me the Witches are going to make all the kids battle each other anyway – only the best will be allowed to fight the Wizards.'

For a moment, staring at that excited angular face, Rachel had a picture of the future: adults probably killed outright, the weakest children pushed aside, the gifted honed into a Wizard-hating elite – led by a handful of the most ruthless children, like Heiki.

No, Rachel thought, thinking of Dad. That mustn't happen.

'Better get on with it,' Heiki said. 'Morpeth and Eric may still be alive, but they can't last much longer.'

'Tell me where they are!'

'No.'

'You will!'

'Make me!'

Attack spells instantly offered themselves. Rachel ignored them. She had to get Heiki away from Mum and find Morpeth's signal! Maybe his scent-tag could be picked up close to the house...

She glanced briefly, agonizingly, at Mum – and shifted.

Nothing happened, and seeing Rachel's bewilderment Heiki laughed. Rachel tried again, suddenly becoming aware of a spell she had never experienced before. It was a *counter-shifting* spell. Heiki was holding her back.

Rachel switched to simpler flight spells and escaped through the kitchen window. She flew into the early dawn sky, swiftly, though not too swiftly until she was certain Heiki followed. Once they were safely past the streets of the town and over open countryside, Rachel decided to really test Heiki's speed. Her fleetest spells took control, yet no matter how rapidly she travelled Heiki kept up effortlessly.

'You don't get away that easily,' Heiki said, smiling. 'I've got a particularly nasty spell I want to try out. It would be a pity not to use it, Rachel, because Calen and I created the spell especially for you. We call it a *multi-signal-hunter-slug*. See what you think.'

'No. Don't...'

Heiki parted her thin lips and blew the hunter at Rachel.

The hunter was alive. Slug-shaped, mottled and black, it wriggled in a methodical manner away from Heiki's mouth. Rachel did not need to ask her spells for protection. They came forward immediately, a complex layering of defences. Frenetically, they sought combinations that might hold off the hunter's threat.

'You can't stop it,' said Heiki. 'Not in time. What are you going to do, Rachel?'

Rachel's information spells investigated the hunter. As it swam towards her head she realized she couldn't evade this weapon, or retreat from it, or ever shift fast enough to avoid its bite. Only one choice, her spells told her: become nothing. A hunter needs a victim.

Become nothing? Rachel wondered. What did that mean? She was flesh and muscle; she breathed, sweated. How could she become nothing?

Flicking its tail the hunter came for her. It was close now.

Rachel – still with Heiki flying alongside – came to a dead-halt in the sky. Heiki and her weapon also stopped. All three were anchored against the mottled clouds, unmoving. For a moment the hunter was perplexed. Then it lunged at Rachel's heart.

Hide! shrieked her spells.

Trying not to panic, Rachel masked the obvious signals. She scattered her magical scent. She disguised her panting frost-white breath. She bleached all colour from her body and even her clothing, until she was virtually transparent, the pale blue sky visible through her face.

Still the hunter came for her.

How can it detect me now? Rachel wondered – then realized how many alternative signs it had to choose from.

Like her heart, her poor hammering heart. Rachel could not prevent the thudding, but she could suppress the tiny vibrations each beat made. She did that. The breeze ruffled her clothes and stirred her hair. Rachel held all the strands stiff, even the finest hair on her wrists. Her eyes were open, dry, needing to blink. She did not blink. Broken light patterns reflected on her eyes from passing clouds. Rachel froze the patterns.

Gradually the hunter slowed. It opened a hot mouth next to her left eye – and waited.

Utter stillness without movement or sound.

The hunter angled left and right, baffled. Where were its signals? Sensing warmth it turned. Here, behind it, was pigmented skin and moist breath and movement.

'No!' wailed Heiki, suddenly understanding.

The hunter was designed to strike without mercy, and Heiki's cry only brought it on more speedily. Before she could fend it off the hunter sank through her legs. It ate deeply, burning through the flesh and bone until her thin ankles were fused together. By the time Heiki had called off its attack the entire lower half of her body was charred and smoking in the cold sky.

Rachel watched, appalled. Then she saw that incredibly Heiki already had the worst burning under control – soon she would be fit enough to continue her spell-making. Rachel quickly shifted, scurrying above the Arctic seas. Putting space between herself and Heiki, she extended her scent flaps, sniffing for any trace of Morpeth's tag.

At last, she found it: a feeble signal – but enough to follow.

Rachel tracked it northwards, shifting over the deep waters of the ocean. If she could smell the trace, did that mean Morpeth was still alive? The signal would probably linger for a while, she realized, whether he was breathing or not. She thought of Eric – and an image of his face, pallid and dead, jumped into her mind. No!

She tore across the ocean.

Heiki was not far behind. While Rachel followed a weak scent, Heiki knew exactly where Morpeth and Eric had been taken. She outflanked her, cutting in giant precise shifts over the Norwegian Sea, and simply waited. She did not bother to hide.

Rachel almost flew into Heiki. Seeing her – just in time – she held a position above the waves and viewed her opponent. Heiki's burnt legs still sizzled and cracked as they contracted in the cold air, but the injuries were mending rapidly. Heiki seemed at ease, strands of her thin white hair blown in all directions by the wind. She opened her palms and Rachel saw new weapons cradled there. Death-spells.

Heiki held them like treasured pets. 'Are you ready for these?'

Rachel beheld Heiki. Her face was contorted with excitement. It was a brutal face – terrifying, almost inhuman. But she *is* human, Rachel reminded herself. To have any chance of finding Eric alive, she knew she had to avoid the death-spells. Even if she could defeat them all, it would take too long. She thought: before a Witch got hold of you, Heiki, you must have behaved differently. There has to be a way to get through to you...

Cautiously, Rachel drifted towards Heiki, opening her hands and mouth to prove she hid no obvious weapons.

'Giving up already?' enquired Heiki.

'No, I've come for a chat.'

Heiki laughed. 'Go on, then.'

'What prize have the Witches offered you for defeating me?'

'Something special.'

'I doubt it,' Rachel said. 'I bet I can guess. They promised to change you, didn't they? They promised to turn plain ordinary Heiki into a Witch.'

Heiki's mouth gaped. 'H-how do you know that?'

'I was offered the same thing, on another world.'

'And you didn't want it?' Heiki was amazed. 'You refused?'

'I didn't like the killing I was expected to do in return.'

Heiki shrugged. 'Only the best survive. No point getting squeamish.'

Rachel studied her closely. 'Why did you order those kids to punish my Mum? She's no contest. Where's the challenge in that?'

'Parents are rubbish,' Heiki said vehemently.

'You don't like them, do you?' Rachel edged closer. 'Why not? What makes you dislike parents so much?'

'No magic. The Witches—'

Rachel cut her off. 'No. It's not that. It's something else, isn't it? What are you holding back?' Heiki appeared suddenly uncomfortable. 'This hatred of adults,' Rachel said, 'it's ... got nothing to do with the Witches, has it?' She leapt in the dark. 'You hated parents *before* the Witches came!'

Heiki said nothing.

'What happened?' Rachel pressed. 'What did yours do that was so awful?'

'I won't tell you anything.'

'Did they hurt you?' Rachel drifted nearer, until they were almost touching. 'No, it isn't that, either. What happened? Can't you tell me? Is it too painful?'

'Shut up!'

'You were *abandoned*, weren't you?'

Heiki flinched, as if she had been struck.

'Shut up!' she screamed.

'Is that what the Witches promised you?' Rachel asked. 'Revenge on adults. Is that what all this is about?' Heiki's face darkened, her lips trembling with emotion. It was then, for the first time, that Rachel saw Heiki for what she truly was: an unwanted teenage girl, encouraged by Calen to hit out at everyone.

'You don't like anybody, do you?' Rachel whispered to her. 'Because no one likes you.'

'How dare—!' began Heiki, then tears burst from her bitter, angry face. The tears came so suddenly and with such energy that Rachel instinctively reached out a hand to console her.

Heiki shrugged it off, keeping her face covered to hide her feelings.

'The Witches like me,' she murmured at last. 'Calen likes me.'

'No,' said Rachel. 'She doesn't. Calen's just playing with you.'

Heiki clenched her eyes, holding back the rest of the

tears. 'I don't want your pity!' she muttered. 'I *am* special. Better than other children. Calen told me so!'

Rachel searched for hope in Heiki's resentful expression – but the brief moment of frailty had gone.

'They'll never make you into a real Witch,' Rachel told her. 'Calen's lying.'

'You're wrong. I'm *already* a Witch!' Heiki caressed her throat and gazed proudly down. A lean grey snake lay against her neck. 'See!'

Rachel studied the infant snake and saw at once that it was a fake. It could barely breathe or hold its ginger eyes open – as if what little life it possessed was already fading. She lifted its limp head, and the snake did not even try to stop her.

'Look at it carefully,' Rachel said. 'Do you really think Calen's soul-snake was ever like this? They've given you a scrawny toy, to keep you happy. A Witch's joke.'

'That's not true,' cried Heiki, her cheeks flushing. 'It's just young and weak because … because it's a baby and my magic's not very powerful yet.'

'There's no link between your magic and this mechanical thing. I'll prove it.'

Rachel cuffed the snake. Its jaw flopped open, and all its snake-colour faded immediately. White and semi-rigid, it lay unmoving in Heiki's hand.

Heiki leapt back, stifling a scream. With great tenderness she examined her snake, delicately rubbing its scales. She breathed on the nostrils, hoping that might bring it back to life. When the snake did not respond she glared at Rachel.

'You've killed it!'

'I didn't,' said Rachel earnestly. 'You saw I hardly touched it. A real soul-snake can defend itself. No living thing dies like this. Why can't you understand?'

'You'll say anything, won't you?' snarled Heiki. 'I was confused. I see what this is all about now. You're just scared to fight!'

'No, believe me,' Rachel implored her. 'That's not—'

'It was just a baby! It needed to learn like me, that's all!' Heiki stroked the snake's flaccid neck longingly. 'I...I might never be given a new one...' She became silent; then her face darkened with controlled anger. 'You had better run, Rachel. Try to find Eric. Go on! It won't make any difference. Even if you reach him before me the troupe will get you anyway. They know your appearance, and your magic scent. I've instructed them to kill on sight.' She smiled ferociously. 'And they do exactly what I tell them.'

'Did—'

'No! I'm not listening! I'll give you a few seconds head start...'

Rachel said, 'Are you sure you want to fight, Heiki? If so, better make sure you don't lose. No mistakes. Calen wouldn't accept that.'

Heiki bent the hardening snake into a curve. Pressing it forcefully against her neck, she uttered a few soothing words to its blank face. Seeing this, Rachel knew that any chance of influencing Heiki had gone. If she enjoys stroking its lifeless body, Rachel thought, perhaps she can never be convinced.

'Two seconds,' said Heiki.

Rachel pulled Heiki towards her – and widened her eyes. Dazzling silver light flashed out. For a moment only, Heiki was caught off guard. Snatching the snake from her neck, Rachel tossed it towards the sea. While Heiki dived after it, Rachel shifted.

A few precious seconds …

She sensed Morpeth was achingly close now. *Where was he!*

Suddenly, a lonely sound – the caw of a gull – followed by the crash of waves against shore.

Land.

Rachel swept across the last of the ocean. A narrow pebble beach lay ahead. Walruses crowded in the surf, and beyond them rose sheer ice cliffs. Rachel flew above their massive height and discovered snow, the beginnings of a vast continent extending north. At first she could see nothing except a remorseless whiteness. Then she noticed green dots. As Rachel closed in the dots widened, gained limbs, became children, dozens of them, plummeting from the sky, attacking two others on the ground.

'Morpeth! Eric!' she screamed.

Flinging herself at them, Rachel dropped beneath the thin cloud. Heiki was behind, closing rapidly, matching Rachel's movements. They swooped down together, so fast that no ordinary human eye could follow their speed.

Rachel made straight for the cluster of children.

But it was Heiki who landed first.

14

VICTIM

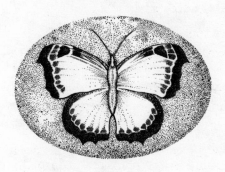

A familiar girl with long black hair strode confidently up to Morpeth.

'Rachel!' Filled with joy, he staggered towards her as best he could.

Another girl landed some distance behind. This one was thin and white-haired, identical to Marshall's eerie description of Heiki. Morpeth shouted:

'Rachel! Can't you see she's behind you!'

Ignoring him, the black-haired girl addressed the troupe. 'Attack her! I showed you how!'

The children wavered, staring uncertainly at each other. Then they leapt straight onto the black-haired girl herself. 'What?' she gasped, trying to get away. Marshall was one of the first to reach her. He swiped her legs, pulling her down. As soon as she hit the snow the whole troupe sprang from all angles, pinning her arms.

'No!' screamed Morpeth. 'Leave her alone!'

Barely able to walk any longer he tottered over, trying to pull them off.

'Eric!' he pleaded. 'Help me!'

Eric raised himself from the snow. Getting to his feet he managed to take a few steps – *away* from the fight.

'What are you doing?' roared Morpeth. 'Get over here!'

Eric ignored him. Gingerly prodding the snow by his feet he found the prapsies. They lay together, a mess of feathers in a snowdrift, stunned and bewildered – though not badly hurt.

'Never mind the prapsies!' Morpeth cried. 'Do something! That's your *sister*!'

Eric continued his thoughtful inspection of the child-birds. He tucked in a few misplaced feathers, tested wing muscles for damage, pinched their rosy cheeks.

'Eric! What are—'

'It's not Rachel,' Eric shushed him. 'Be quiet, will you.'

To Morpeth the girl looked exactly like Rachel, even possessed her distinctive magical scent. 'Surely…'

'Trust me,' Eric murmured.

Cross-legged, the white-haired girl sat in the snow, staying out of the fight.

For the first time Morpeth gazed closely at her. She gazed back, forcing out a meagre half-smile. The face was wrong, but Morpeth knew that smile. He turned back in astonishment to the dark-haired girl. Not Rachel, he realized – Heiki.

A *switch* of appearances.

The troupe had been completely fooled. They engulfed Heiki. As Morpeth watched, for one extraordinary moment she held them off. Dragging herself upright, kicking at the grasping hands, Heiki hauled herself across the snow and tried to get away. But before her dazed mind could make a shifting spell – or even begin to understand what Rachel had done – the troupe leapt on her again, and slammed her into the ground. They did not stop to think about what damage they were doing. Terror drove them. Somewhere close, in the sky above, Calen observed. She would punish any hesitation. And Heiki also looked on.

They could see her not far away, calmly expecting her orders to be followed. Hadn't she demanded they be ruthless? The children followed her orders well, using fists and feet and spells. Amidst the snow turning to grey slush, they continued on and on with an incessant mechanical battering, waiting to be told by Heiki or Calen to stop.

Morpeth pleaded with the white-haired girl, 'Rachel, surely that's enough!'

Tears streamed down her pale blue eyes, and it was odd to see those soft wet tears against that hard brittle face.

'Nearly. I can't take any chances,' she whispered. 'You've no idea how strong Heiki is.'

When several seconds passed containing no sounds at all except the crunch of fists, Rachel undid the reversal spells, and shouted: 'Stop!'

The real Rachel, her hair dark and flowing in the wind, sat in the snow. At first the troupe could not understand what they were seeing. Their minds fought against believing it. Finally the truth sank in and their arms no longer came up and down on the girl beneath. Stumbling, crawling, desperate to get away, they peeled off Heiki.

Rachel lowered her face – not wanting to see what they had done.

The children formed a wide circle, surrounding Heiki. She did not need all the room they offered. A small heap against the reddening snow, she lay spread out in all her injury.

'Is she ... alive?' Paul asked.

'Yes!' rasped Heiki, her voice strangled. Somehow she found the strength to dig an elbow in the slush and prop herself partially up. All the children retreated further away – despite Heiki's appalling wounds they were still frightened of her.

'Get me up,' she demanded.

The children wavered uncertainly, many looking at Rachel for guidance.

'If you ... don't ...' Heiki said between short gasping breaths, 'I will make sure ... the Witches ... kill ... you all ... I ...' Her face slipped to the ground. 'Help me,' she begged, sounding suddenly pitiful.

A few children, led by Paul, started walking towards Rachel.

As soon as she saw this Calen burst from the sky. With a single claw she plucked Marshall and two other children by their necks and hoisted them into the air.

'You timid maggots!' she cried, addressing all the children. 'Follow me!' She pointed at Heiki. 'Except her. Leave her here.'

The older members of the troupe, many glancing despairingly at Rachel, raised their arms and flew into the air. Slowly they fell in behind Calen, following her northwards.

'Can't we do anything to keep them here?' Eric called across to Rachel.

'Let them go,' she answered dejectedly. 'I'm too weak to do anything now. So are you.'

'I'm not too weak.'

'You can hardly stand up, Eric.'

He tried – and collapsed when his frozen knees refused to lift him. The prapsies covered his hands, trying to warm them with their downy feathers.

In small groups, the remaining children rose from the snows. They picked up the four children whose flying spells Eric had destroyed and formed a sad, bedraggled line across the sky. The youngest were the most reluctant to leave. Bunching together, they clung tightly to Rachel's side and squeezed between her legs. Finally even these toddlers lost their nerve. Holding hands they glided off together, pointing their mournful eyes towards the Pole.

'Why won't they stay?' Eric muttered in frustration. 'Surely they realize nothing good's waiting for them out there!'

'Of course they do,' said Rachel. 'But they know I'm not strong enough to directly challenge all the Witches. What else can they do except follow Calen and hope they don't get punished too much?'

None of the children had stayed behind to assist Heiki. Fitfully, like a bird trying to make it home on a single ruined wing, she managed to flap awkwardly on her left arm. The right arm was dislocated, hanging limply by her side.

An easy victim, Rachel thought. A single spell would be enough to finish her off now.

'Well?' Eric asked. 'Are you going to let Heiki escape, after what she's done?'

Rachel's voice shook with emotion. 'There'll *always* be another Heiki somewhere,' she whispered. 'Should I kill everyone who comes after me? What about all those kids who've been in contact with Witches already. They're a danger, aren't they? Isn't that what Heiki would do – hunt them down just in case they're a threat?'

Eric did not reply.

Morpeth shuffled up to Rachel and held her tightly. Together they watched Heiki pass overhead like a broken shadow.

'I'll help you,' Rachel called up to her. 'Let me.'

'No,' rasped Heiki. 'I don't want your help. I'll make it back on my own.'

'Even if you do, what kind of welcome do you think Calen will offer?'

Heiki said nothing, trying to heave her body further up the sky. The troupe were a long way ahead, leaving her ever further behind as they gradually dwindled, fading against the brightness of the Arctic morning.

'I can't believe Heiki's trying to make it back to the troupe,' Eric said. 'Not after Calen did nothing to help her.'

'She's never faced a Witch's punishments,' Morpeth said quietly. 'She has no idea what Calen will do to her.'

And then, overhead, he heard the flutter of wings.

'A whirling baby!' marvelled a prapsy.

It was Yemi, clinging to his butterflies. All this time he had been waiting patiently for Calen. Where was she going with the children who made the shouting noises? They frightened him, and he was worried they might hurt Calen. As Calen flew away, he stayed quiet and still, as he had promised, but he felt scared. Then he noticed a familiar magic on the ground below. It filled him with the happiest of feelings. He floated down to greet it.

Rachel stood in the snow, surrounded by Yemi's Camberwell Beauties. They circled her, landing on her head, making the prapsies nervous. Two of the largest, their wings revolving like helicopter blades, carried Yemi himself gently down.

Rachel held out her arms.

But before Yemi reached her a warning shriek made the escorting butterflies cover his eyes. It was Calen. Leaving the other children she raced across the sky, calling Yemi's name over and over. Some of his butterflies waved their antennae excitedly at Calen; most hovered closer to Rachel.

'Come, Yemi!' Calen yelled. 'Don't make me angry.'

He hung uneasily just out of reach of Rachel's hands. Some of his Beauties pulled his toes towards her; others tugged him towards Calen. Yemi looked longingly at them both.

'Don't struggle over him,' Morpeth warned Rachel. 'You're too weary to fight Calen.'

'I know,' Rachel whispered – yet she could not stop herself. She opened her arms even wider, inviting Yemi inside. He sank lower, more certain, giggling at his butterflies.

As he touched Rachel's outstretched fingers a smell came over the wind, from the direction of Calen. It was a female smell – sweet, faintly musky – and palpably human: the smell of his mother.

Deeply confused, Yemi glanced at Rachel, then Calen, his butterflies flapping uneasily about the sky.

'Yemi, come.' It was his mother's gruff voice, emerging from Calen's four mouths.

'That's not your mother,' Rachel said.

Calen shifted. She reappeared as a faraway speck at the front of the troupe, leaving the powerful scent of mother lingering behind. 'Follow me!' she called.

'Mama!' Yemi wailed. 'Mama!'

'No!' Rachel cried. She projected a new smell – the scent of Fola, mingled with cornflower and other smells of his home she recalled. 'Go to your sister,' she insisted. 'Remember, Yemi! Go to your real home! Go home!'

For a few seconds Yemi's soft brown eyes blinked at Rachel. Then, without a glance at Calen this time, he shifted. It was a single immense shift that instantly placed him thousands of miles south. Rachel clapped her hands in joy, knowing where he had gone – and looked defiantly across the sky at Calen.

'A small victory!' Calen conceded. 'How long do you think Yemi's dull family can keep him occupied? He'll return to me soon enough.' She turned her back on Rachel and continued to lead the ragged troupe north.

Eric was still reeling from the sheer magnitude of Yemi's shifting spell. He had never felt such awesome power or control, even from Dragwena.

'That was no ordinary shift,' he said. 'Yemi didn't just use his own magic. He used the magic of the troupe kids to help him.'

Rachel shook her head. 'No, that's not possible. Even a Witch can't do that.'

'Well, he did,' insisted Eric. 'He took what he wanted. A bit from every child, not too much. Not greedy. Just what he needed.'

'Yemi's peculiarly gifted, isn't he?' Morpeth said. 'His magic seems completely distinctive, unlike that of other children.'

'In every way,' Eric said. 'His spells are weird. They're not like yours or Rachel's, or Witches', either.'

For one magnificent second Rachel thought of Larpskendya. She trembled, the possibility too wonderful to bear.

'More like a Wizard?' she said, hardly daring to ask. 'Is his magic like Larpskendya's?'

'No,' Eric sighed. 'It's not Larpskendya, Rachel. That baby's magic is not like *anything* we've seen before.'

As the last of the children ebbed over the horizon with Calen, Eric rummaged in his bulging, lively coat.

'Hiya, boys!'

The prapsies beamed merrily out of the pockets.

Eric's hands were too numb to feel the touch of their feathers. One prapsy rubbed the side of its delicate head against his fingers.

'Flipping heck!' it said, licking them distastefully.

The other prapsy rolled its eyes. 'Oh, don't be fussy. It's still Eric.'

'I know, but he's ice pops. You're so moody!'

'Shut up, you dinky warbler!'

'Ugly, cutted lips!'

'Are my lips cutted?' A sorrowful eye turned to Eric for reassurance.

He rubbed both prapsies' cheeks with his coat sleeve, not wanting to touch them with his cold fingers. 'They are cutted,' he said, 'but they look good, boys. In fact, you both look great. You *are* great: like eagles.'

The prapsies crooned delightedly.

'Time to sort out your frostbite, goldilocks,' Rachel said.

Eric smiled. 'Do the old man first. Age before beauty.'

'Don't these hurt?' She examined his swollen fingers.

He grinned. 'Can't feel a thing.'

'I suppose that's because you're tough?'

'Dead right.'

Rachel repaired the worst of Eric's frostbite. The spells needed were basic enough, but she was tired, so it took some time to finish. Then she attended to Morpeth.

'Save your strength,' he objected.

'For what?' she said huskily. 'What's more important than this?'

Morpeth's back was deeply bruised where he had taken

on most of the blows aimed at Eric. Rachel anaesthetized the stinging and carefully mended the worst of the broken blood vessels. Finally she wrapped everyone inside an insulating warmth even the stabbing Arctic winds could not pierce.

For a while they simply gazed northwards, feeling hungry and weary and anxious.

'What a miserable place this is,' Eric said. He shaded his eyes, trying to find any details in the whiteness stretching eternally ahead. 'I bet the Witches love it.'

Rachel explained what had occurred at the house. 'If you want, I can take you back home,' she said seriously. 'It will be safer there.'

Eric shook his head. 'No way. I don't want to give the Witches or anyone else a reason to go after Mum again.' He kicked the snows in frustration. 'Damn! Where's Larpskendya?'

'He'll come,' Rachel said tightly. 'He will come.'

'If we want to find the Witch-base we need to follow the children quickly,' Morpeth told them. 'Before their scent fades or is masked.'

'Brilliant,' Eric muttered resignedly. 'I can't wait to meet all five Witches!'

Morpeth gazed at both of them. 'There is an alternative. We could try to find a quiet place to hide and survive, until Larpskendya arrives.'

'No,' Rachel said. 'That will leave all children at the Witches' mercy.' She thought of Paul, and wondered how long it would take Calen to finally crush his spirit. 'I'm not just letting the Witches do what they want any more,' she

THE SCENT OF MAGIC

said. 'We must at least try to find out where their base is.'

All three stared northwards, steeling themselves to go on. The wind had picked up, and with it came a light snowfall, squalling into their faces.

'I can still detect Heiki's scent,' Eric remarked. 'She's wounded, leaving a big trail of magic. It's, well, *leaking* out of her.'

Rachel sent out her information spells. When they returned, she found unexpected tears welling in her eyes. 'Heiki's falling further and further behind,' she said. 'She's attempting so hard to keep up, but she can't. Her injuries are too bad to repair this time.'

'Does she think we're coming after her?' Eric asked.

'It's nothing to do with us,' murmured Rachel. 'She's still trying to impress the Witches. Heiki's doing everything she can to hide her weakness, especially from Calen.'

Eric frowned. 'Why bother? Hasn't that Witch already given up on her?'

Rachel shared a look of understanding with Morpeth. On Ithrea it had taken all of her willpower to resist the allure of Dragwena. And she had only needed to resist for a few days. Heiki had spent far longer with the Witches, being made to feel utterly special.

Poor Heiki had fallen half in love with Calen's glamour.

15

ARRIVALS

Heiki hauled her frail body towards the Pole.

She was too weak to shift. While she still had the strength she flew. When that left her she limped on ankles that had never fully recovered from the hunter. Finally she crawled. It took her over an hour to make the last few windswept yards to the perimeter of the Witch-base.

Calen met her. She stared contemptuously.

'Why have you returned? There is only more punishment for you here.'

Heiki knelt shamefully in the snow. 'Please help me. Please. I am in pain...'

'You failed,' said Calen. 'There are no second chances for a failed Witch.'

'I'll do anything,' Heiki promised. 'I'm still willing. Don't give up on me.'

'I asked you to make me proud. You could not even do that.'

'Please. Give me another chance.'

'No. There is no chance for you now.'

Calen clenched Heiki's scalp and carried her like an unwanted bag between the towers.

'What's going to happen to me?'

Calen did not reply. Seeing Heiki fiddling with the baby snake, she snatched it from her neck and tossed its hardened body to the ground. Heiki started to cry. She tried not to, but she couldn't stop the flow, and was too weary to wipe the wetness away.

She gazed up at Calen. 'Am I ... to be killed?'

'Do you even need to ask?'

Calen flew to her own eye-tower and dumped Heiki inside.

Later Calen was summoned by her mother.

Nervously, she made her way to Heebra's vast tower, expecting to be severely punished for Heiki's failure. Nylo squirmed against her throat.

Heebra stood gazing out of the eye-window. For several minutes she ignored Calen. Eventually she said, 'Heiki, your favourite, the child you personally trained, was defeated.'

Calen bowed her head in humiliation.

'You were also mistaken about the other children on this world,' said Heebra. 'They can be instructed, but many are defiant or unpredictable.'

'If I have more time ...'

'More time!' screamed Heebra. She turned to face her daughter. 'It will take an *age* to forge the children into an army loyal enough to threaten the Wizards!'

'Then—' faltered Calen, holding Nylo close, 'do you recommend ... we leave?'

Heebra's four jaws twisted from anger to amusement. 'Leave this marvellous world to the Wizards? I think not. No. A new plan: we will drag Larpskendya here as fast as we can!'

'I don't understand.'

'Larpskendya has always been the great prize,' Heebra said. 'I've always known that if we could kill him we could quickly crush the Order of Wizards. For the first time I have an advantage. When the two girls battled I reopened the channel between Rachel and Larpskendya. He cannot communicate, but he sees everything that frightens his preferred child, sees with her eyes.' Heebra smiled. 'Heiki served her purpose. I always knew Rachel would defeat her. However, even their little skirmish will have horrified the gentle Larpskendya.'

'Surely he will be too cautious to come.'

'No,' Heebra said. 'He will come for his Rachel, count on it. A scout report has already reached me that he is rushing here to protect his cherished Witch-slayer.'

Calen's mouths widened. 'Are we ready? Larpskendya will not be alone.'

'He *is* alone!' exulted Heebra. 'The Griddas have accomplished far more than I ever expected, Calen. We sent them over a wide area. The Wizards needed to scatter to confront them. Larpskendya is presently isolated, with no companions to hold his hand.' She drew Mak against the skin of her nostrils and sniffed his ripe fragrance. 'Best of all, Calen, Larpskendya is injured. A Gridda slashed him at the Leppos world! I've made sure others in the area have orders to harry and harm him all the journey to Earth. Our Griddas won't allow him to recover. When Larpskendya arrives he will be exhausted.'

'Will he?' Calen said uncertainly. 'His power is immense. Even with your capability amongst us, are we enough with only four other Witches...'

'Only four?' Heebra laughed. 'Good. Then you did not detect the coming of the rest. In that case I'm sure Larpskendya will not have done so, either.'

'The rest?' Calen glanced round.

'I summoned them as soon as I realized how to set the trap.'

At a gesture from Heebra hundreds of High Witches suddenly appeared. They packed the sky with their magnificence, their black dresses streaming in the breeze. Seeing Calen's surprise, most were amused.

'How many?' Calen gasped.

'Seven hundred and fifty-six of our best. They just arrived, fresh and itching to fight. Take control of them, Calen. Let those who wish it start building their own eye-towers, but make sure all the new sisters remain hidden. Rachel expects to find only five Witches. She should continue to believe that. We must have no mistakes now.'

'Larpskendya is bound to suspect a trap,' Calen said. 'He will be cautious, survey the position, and not show himself until he is ready.'

'Agreed. So we must make him desperate. When Rachel sees the fun I have planned for the other children here, Larpskendya will dash the final distance. That will draw the last reserves from him.'

'What fun?' asked Calen, intrigued.

'I want you to create a single prison, isolate the children there and panic them, while Rachel watches.'

'Panic them? How?'

'Start by executing Heiki,' said Heebra. 'I want to make a special example of her. If her death does not bring Larpskendya move onto another child – any child, I don't care who.'

Calen nodded. 'How do you want me to execute Heiki?'

'As you wish,' said Heebra. 'Wait. A better idea. Choose something – a device – all children will recognize, no matter where they are from.'

'One of their own kind of murder machines?'

'Or something even simpler, perhaps. Talk to the youngest children. Find out what kind of games they share or like to play, and use something from those to frighten them. It's fear we want now, Calen. Build it up. Terrify all these children, and let Rachel witness it. Make Larpskendya hurry the final stretch.'

'And later? How will we dispose of Rachel?'

'After I've used her to capture Larpskendya we'll both deal with her, each in our own way.'

Calen left the eye-tower to carry out her orders.

Heebra glided across the chamber and seated herself. From the height of her meticulously shrouded eye-tower she could observe everything for dozens of miles. Rachel, Eric and Morpeth approached within a primitive spell. Heebra knew exactly where they were. She had deliberately drawn the Witches and all the polar bears away from their perimeter guard to ensure that the children came all the way into the base. The trap was almost complete.

For the first time since arriving on Earth Heebra permitted herself to relax completely. The view outside pleased her more and more. Snow rarely fell in this part of the world, but it did not melt. Her Witches could make a home here with little difficulty. The first stage would be to replace the disgusting sunlight with Ool's sensuous darkness. Next they would make the snows pour eternally.

But such matters could wait. With enormous anticipation Heebra imagined Larpskendya tearing through space, consumed with tiredness and injury, seeing through Rachel's eyes, trying to arrive in time to stop the bloodshed.

But he would not stop it. Not this time. This time she and hundreds of her most superb High Witches were ready for him.

16

IMPRISONMENT

Within a cloaking spell Rachel, Morpeth, Eric and the prapsies followed Heiki. They observed her meeting with Calen. Without realizing it, they entered the Witch perimeter watched by hundreds of pairs of tattooed eyes.

'This could be Ithrea,' said Eric. His voice was barely audible.

'You don't need to whisper,' Rachel told him. 'Our voices can't be heard.'

'I'll whisper anyway.'

The prapsies would not settle. Constantly twitching, they rolled their eyes and tasted the falling snow with suspicious pink tongues.

'Why are they fidgeting so much?' Rachel asked Eric.

'They're jumpy, that's all.'

One prapsy sniffed the air. 'A Witch, maybe.'

The other puckered its lips. 'Spine-gutters!'

'Shush, boys, I'll look after you,' Eric promised, petting their feathers.

'No, listen to them,' Morpeth said. 'Remember they spent hundreds of years on Ithrea as Dragwena's pets.' He stroked their neck feathers. 'How many Witches? Can you tell?'

'We see them stinkers!'

Morpeth nodded impatiently. 'But how many?'

'Many!'

'Too many to count?'

Both prapsies peered shrewdly upwards. 'See there!' They covered their faces.

Ahead, the Witch towers had appeared. There were five of them, each over four hundred feet tall, arranged in a faultless circle. Harsh emerald light radiated from the eye-windows, easily penetrating the meagre snowfall.

'There's no cover for us out here,' Morpeth said. 'We daren't get any closer.'

'To see what's happening we must,' Rachel insisted.

Cautiously she drew them towards the nearest tower. Her spells begged her not to. They wanted her to survive. They told her to shift. They pleaded with her to disguise herself, abandon Eric and Morpeth, and just get away. Rachel pressed on, ignoring their increasingly frantic warnings.

In an area of flat undisturbed snow between the towers, they stopped.

'Gutters!' squealed both prapsies.

For the first time the Witches showed themselves. Clothed in their skin-tight black dresses, three soared between the eye-windows, entering and leaving so swiftly that their bodies appeared to be inescapably everywhere at once. One Witch, Calen, passed directly over Rachel. She did not look down.

'They can't see us,' Rachel said, trying to reassure herself.

'Or they're pretending not to,' suggested Morpeth.

Eric spotted a new structure. 'What's that? It wasn't there earlier.'

A rough building made from ice was beginning to form inside the ring of the eye-towers. It was three stories high – and growing. Two Witches made short flights around the structure, relaying orders. As floor after floor took shape, Morpeth could not understand how the building was being constructed. Then he saw the meaning of the blurs scrabbling across the slabs of ice.

'The children are making it!'

Dozens were at work. Supervised by the Witches, the children used their hands and magic to compact the snow into blocks of ice. They moved at speed, shaping the walls and ceilings, taunted by the Witches, who allowed them no rest. Morpeth, Eric and Rachel watched in awe as the entire building was completed in less than an hour.

'What's it for?' Eric asked.

Morpeth said, 'It's obviously purpose-built, not made to live inside. Some kind of . . . prison. See how cramped it is? Each room is just big enough for a child to stand up in, with a single window. And notice: all the windows point in one direction only – towards *us*.'

Rachel shuddered. Was that a coincidence? It had to be...

'They've finished,' Eric said. 'What now?'

'Wait,' Rachel answered.

The Witches drove the children to their appointed rooms. They stood at the empty frames of their ice windows, gazing mournfully down.

At first Rachel thought the children were looking directly at her. Then she realized they were peering down the walls. At the base of the ice prison two Witches waited either side of a small doorway. One was Calen. She opened the door – and a figure shuffled out.

It was a girl, still badly injured: Heiki.

She stumbled forward, hauling numerous pieces of wood and a length of rope across the snow.

'What is it?' Eric tried to make out the shapes.

'I don't know.' Rachel strained to determine a purpose. 'The parts are so heavy. She can hardly carry them, even using her magic.'

Morpeth gazed around at the pinched, nervous faces of the children. 'They've been told what's going to happen,' he said, suddenly understanding. 'Each child has a perfect view.'

Eric frowned. 'A perfect view for what?'

'To witness whatever's planned for Heiki. To watch the spectacle.'

Once or twice Heiki dropped her load or tried to rest. Each time Calen flew over and struck her ankles, forcing her to move on. Eventually she hoisted herself far enough away from the foot of the prison for all the children to have a clear view. Calen hissed instructions in her ear.

Nodding, Heiki, piece by piece, erected a device.

'Oh no,' said Eric, recognizing it. 'No, please.'

It was a Hangman.

Rachel shuddered, almost fell. She had prepared herself for many things, but not this. Pity for Heiki poured through her – and dread. At the same time her shifting spells automatically leapt forward – awaiting a command to leave.

Heiki finished making the angular base and frame. Pausing a moment, she raised the length of rope from the snow and attached it to the Hangman. Calen tested the rope's resistance by making Heiki jerk it several times. Then Calen folded the rope into the shape of a noose, picked Heiki up and used her head to measure the size needed. Rachel numbly tried devising a defence, but against five High Witches her spells offered nothing that would work.

Get away! Get away! they screamed.

The Hangman was complete. Heiki leaned heavily against the base, and as she stared up at the knotted rope any resolve she had left faded. She covered her face and wept. All this time she had still been trying to impress Calen. Knowing the Witches never respond to pity, she kept her chin up, hoping the defiant attitude Calen had once so liked might make a difference. But Calen gave her no encouragement, and, now that the Hangman was waiting for her, Heiki fell to her knees. She pressed her lips to the black hem of Calen's dress and pleaded.

'Please. Please don't—'

'No second chances,' Calen reminded her. She lifted

Heiki by the scalp, displaying her to the children in the ice building. When Heiki squirmed to pull away, Calen simply tightened her grip.

Morpeth glanced at the rest of the children. From the windows all their haunted eyes were on Heiki, including the youngest. They were obviously being forced to watch. Paul and Marshall stood in adjacent rooms, their expressions petrified.

'Stop this,' Morpeth muttered. 'Rachel, somehow ... we must ...'

Rachel nodded wildly. She had no idea how.

Calen raised Heiki's thin neck towards the noose.

'Listen to me,' Eric whispered. 'Calen is using two spells to control the rope. I've worked them out. I think I can destroy both. Rachel, if you try—'

Morpeth tapped him on the shoulder.

'Rachel,' Eric went on, 'if you attack Calen at the same time, I'll—'

Morpeth tapped him again.

'What!'

Eric felt the hairs on his neck tingle.

Above them, winking from the sky, the Wizards had arrived.

17

the trap

They came in a great stately procession: twenty Wizards.

Singly they came, unfolding from the clouds in majestic robes of crimson and turquoise and burnished gold. And as they came they announced their names in jubilation:

'Areglion! Tournallat! Hensult! Serpantha! ...'

The names meant nothing to the children, but the Witches shrank back. A stupefied Calen stepped away from the Hangman.

'Mother!' she screamed at the sky. 'You promised only Larpskendya!'

Hensult and Serpantha took up positions at the epicentre of the sky. They were shaped like men but taller, as tall as the Witches. Impassively they waited, until the air sang in a manner that tortured the recessed ears of the Witches.

A final cream-robed Wizard had arrived. His many-coloured eyes were untamed.

'Larpskendya!' Rachel cried joyfully, her heart lurching as she took in the sight of him.

For a moment the Great Wizard acknowledged her gravely. Then he and the other Wizards shifted, unfurling in the snow beside Heiki.

Larpskendya picked her shaking body from the Hangman. He wiped away her tears.

Heiki had expected punishment. When Larpskendya simply took her in his strong arms she found herself unable to think clearly. He held her, without words, until she stopped trembling. He touched her injured arm, mending it. At last Heiki gazed up, but she could not meet his eyes. She could barely speak.

'Why…are you helping me?'

Larpskendya seemed surprised. 'Why wouldn't I?'

'After what I've done…'

'Haven't you been punished enough? Do you want more punishment?'

'No,' she murmured. 'Oh…but I've done some terrible things.'

'And you might have done worse,' he answered firmly. 'There is a harder trial ahead, because of you. Will you help me, Heiki?'

Before she could say anything Calen's voice rang out. She had recovered from the entrance of the Wizards, though Nylo still cowered against her throat.

'Twenty Wizards,' she shouted. 'Twenty is not enough.

What is the largest number of Witches you can defeat in personal combat, Larpskendya? Five? Fifty?'

She raised a claw – and one hundred recently built eye-towers shimmered against the sky. Witches soared from them, drawing short curved daggers from their black dresses.

If Larpskendya's Wizards were afraid they did not show it.

'Not impressed?' said Calen. 'A few more, then.'

Exactly six hundred and fifty-six further towers appeared.

Witches swarmed from the eye-windows, so many that their weaving bodies cast half the snow in shadow. Morpeth strained his neck. He could not see beyond the Witches. They crowded all around him, and above him, bathed in luminous green light.

Eric gaped in despair at the sky. 'I don't think even Larpskendya can beat this many,' he whispered, poking the prapsies deep inside his coat. 'We're going to have to fight, too.'

'Wait for a sign,' Rachel said, squeezing his hand. 'Larpskendya will show us what to do.'

The Witches took up rehearsed battle positions in the sky, coming together in packs that surrounded the Wizards. Each pack contained only blood-related sisters – the most ferocious fighting combination. When they were set, each Witch's soul-snake licked diagonally across her face – the traditional signal of battle readiness.

But they did not attack.

Larpskendya was still calm. 'Do your worst, Witch,' he said to Calen, 'as your kind always will. We are prepared.'

He linked hands with the other Wizards, placing Heiki inside the circle they made.

'Perhaps Rachel and her friends would like to join in,' said Calen brightly.

The cloaking spell was laid bare, exposing Rachel, Eric and Morpeth. The children in the building stared in amazement. The Witches merely seemed amused.

'Stay where you are,' Larpskendya warned Rachel.

He consulted with his companion Wizards and said a few urgent words to Heiki. Briefly she argued with him. Then she sneaked a distraught glance at Rachel and started walking across the snow towards her.

'I can't believe it!' Eric blasted. 'Flipping heck, Larpskendya's sent Heiki here. To us!'

'Let her come,' said Rachel, meeting Larpskendya's steady gaze. 'He obviously can't protect her if he has to fight so many.'

'Are *we* going to protect her?' Eric asked defiantly. 'After what she did!'

Heiki shuffled across the snow. Her head was lowered. Unable to bring herself to stand alongside Rachel, she took a position instead awkwardly next to Morpeth. Rachel nodded curtly, showing that she tolerated Heiki's presence, nothing more. Conflicting feelings flooded her. Larpskendya wanted this, but could she trust Heiki?

The Wizards drew closer, standing back to back.

'Are you sure you want this fight?' Larpskendya thundered at Calen. 'Most of your High Witches are here. Even if you defeat us, how many of you will be left to defend Ool against the Griddas? I cannot believe Heebra was foolish enough to let them loose.'

Calen laughed. 'Tell her that yourself. A final surprise!'

All the Witches joined in her mirth, dispersing to leave a gap in the air.

Inside Eric's coat pockets the prapsies began whimpering. It was a sound they had never made before.

'What is it?' said Rachel, trying to decide how to aid the Wizards.

Eric caught his breath. 'Can't you … can't you feel it?'

The whimpers of the prapsies rose in pitch, became screeches.

Rachel could sense the reason clearly now – a huge outbulging of magic.

'Here it comes,' said Eric, clenching his teeth.

In one movement everyone – Witches, Wizards and children – looked up.

Across half the sky a new tower had appeared. It was so immense that all the children had to turn their heads to take in its scope. Rachel found her gaze drawn to the eye-window. A bulky shadow moved behind the glass. For a moment the shadow turned towards her. It moved – then stopped – then looked directly at Rachel. Under its detailed inspection Rachel could not breathe. She had faced Dragwena's death-spells with more equanimity than she now faced this shadow. It could kill her effortlessly, she realized. And it wished to. How it wanted to harm her!

She managed to turn her head.

Slightly, almost imperceptibly, she saw Larpskendya's whole body shiver. Rachel knew then that whatever owned this shadow, he had not anticipated it.

Heebra, leader of the Sisterhood of Ool, burst from the

tower. In a single leap she covered the distance to the Wizards. For a few seconds she merely stood by Larpskendya's side, enjoying his discomfiture. Then she bowed and said, courteously:

'Greetings, Larpskendya. Flesh to flesh at last. I have waited for this.' She examined his shining robe and the other Wizards. 'Shall we dispense with these illusions?'

As she touched his shoulder all the other Wizards vanished. Larpskendya was alone in the snow, his robe shredded. Heebra sniffed. 'Is this tattered mess, this rag, really the celebrated Larpskendya? I expected better. Did you hope to dazzle my Witches into submission with your trick? Or simply divert their attacks?'

Larpskendya was silent. His shoulders slumped, and for the first time Rachel noticed the appalling nature of his real injuries. Three deep slashes crossed his throat. They had clearly been made by a Witch's claws, though much bigger claws than any Rachel had seen before. The wounds were recent, still bleeding.

'I see my Griddas occupied you well,' Heebra said. 'But I knew you would survive. You were always a worthy opponent, Larpskendya.'

'I am not your enemy,' he answered.

'You have killed Witches,' said Heebra. 'Do you deny it?'

'Only when they gave me no choice. I took no pleasure in it.'

'A pity,' said Heebra, laughing. 'You should have done. I will certainly take pleasure in *your* death.' She prodded his neck injury. 'You took the life of my daughter. How long should I make you suffer for that?'

Larpskendya said nothing, knowing no words would make a difference.

'You will not retreat inside your silence,' Heebra told him. 'I have dawdled long enough on this world. I've a desire to commit some violence, and for you to witness it.'

'It is my death you want,' Larpskendya replied evenly. 'Leave the children.'

'It will take more than your death to satisfy me. I think I will kill all the children here. Their lives mean nothing to me.'

'Spare them,' Larpskendya said. 'If you do, I will submit.'

'You would surrender? Without a fight?' She sounded amazed.

'*If* you promise not to harm the children.'

Eric screamed, 'Don't believe her! Larpskendya, what are you doing? She'll kill us anyway!'

'Trust him,' Rachel whispered, never taking her gaze off Larpskendya.

Heebra hesitated. Obviously Larpskendya was protecting the children, as she knew he would, but she had not expected such a simple surrender. She gazed curiously at him. Even in his weakened condition, she knew, Larpskendya could probably destroy hundreds of her best Witches before they overpowered him. The Witch-packs could not wait to fight, but it suited Heebra to avoid conflict. Test his resolve, she thought. If this is another trick like his fake Wizards, expose it.

'Very well,' she said. 'I agree to your terms. Dragwena's blood-honour must be satisfied first, of course. So, I will spare all the children except two. Give me Eric and Rachel. That is *my* condition.'

There was silence. Larpskendya's expression was unreadable.

'Yes,' he murmured at last. 'Do as you wish with Rachel and Eric.'

Most children could not believe this answer. They gazed at him in shock. Several of those imprisoned in the ice prison wept. Eric began shouting insults at Larpskendya at the top of his voice, and the prapsies joined in. Morpeth was stunned, unable to accept what he had heard. Even Heiki shook her head, her emotions in turmoil. At least, if Heebra kept her promise, she might now live through this...

Only Rachel kept her gaze on Larpskendya. She stared at him, her faith unwavering, and he stared back, his gaze filled with determination and asking for her courage.

'Do you promise to obey my Witches?' Heebra asked, a green nail under Larpskendya's chin. 'You will not resist?'

'I will not resist.'

Heebra gestured for the Witches guarding the imprisoned children to empty the ice-structure, and Larpskendya permitted himself to be led inside. Heebra warily surveyed the skies, prepared for a trap. Could she have missed something?

'Take him to the top,' she ordered. 'Hurry. And bind him hard.'

Over a third of the Witches escorted Larpskendya into the prison. At first, most were too nervous to touch him. When he continued to offer no resistance the Witches grew bolder. They bound his wrists and ankles. They fastened his mouth with spell-thread, preventing any utterance of spells. As soon as this was done the ecstatic Witches lost any fear they still had. Snarling with joy, they hauled Larpskendya up the stairway, dragging him against the ice steps to the summit. Faster and faster up the floors they rushed, and as they moved they tightened the spell-bindings until Larpskendya bled.

Rachel was unable to watch.

'Oh, Larpskendya,' Eric said, his anger spent, replaced by a feeling of utter desolation and emptiness. 'What have you done?'

Calen flew up to the Great Wizard's window and placed the edge of her curved dagger against his throat. She trembled with excitement.

'Let me!' she cried.

'No,' said Heebra. 'Let him see his favourites die, first. Start with the girl.'

Morpeth searched for anything with which to defend Eric and Rachel. He glanced at the assembled children. A ragged bunch, they huddled disconsolately in the snow. Morpeth appealed silently to Paul and Marshall. They saw him and averted their eyes. Ashamed, Morpeth realized, too afraid to risk the punishment of the Witches.

'We have a Witch-slayer amongst us,' said Heebra. 'Who wants to fight Rachel?'

Hundreds of Witches clamoured to be noticed. Heebra picked the first ten at random. Those chosen assembled in a semicircle, awaiting Heebra's signal to begin.

Morpeth immediately moved in front of Rachel. Eric took up a position behind, guarding her back. He tried to shoo the prapsies away, but they remained in his pockets, thrusting their soft mouths at Heebra.

'Come on then, you ugly hags!' Eric bellowed. 'As many as you like!'

'Wait,' said a voice.

It was Heiki. Her ashen, thin face shook with fear as she walked the short distance across to Rachel. When she was by Rachel's side, she turned to face Heebra – not calmly, but she faced her. She fumbled for a wrist, and Rachel clutched it.

Morpeth brought their hands together, and drew all four close: a fragile shield.

Heebra lifted a claw to start the attack, but a faint noise on the breeze distracted her. It was such an odd sound in that dread-filled atmosphere that everyone noticed it.

The sound of giggling.

Yemi had arrived. Floating between the Witch towers he swished back and forth as if nothing could be more entrancing. As he closed on the children guarded by the Witches he showed them a new dance he had learned: upright, jigging on his toes, waving his arms. His Camberwell Beauties jigged with him.

'What's he doing here?' Heebra growled at her daughter.

'I...don't understand,' Calen apologized. 'I didn't summon the boy. He should be with his family. I left countless spells to hold him there.'

'Remove him!' said Heebra, gazing suspiciously at Larpskendya.

Calen flew from the prison to intercept Yemi, but she

could not catch him. Each time she reached out her claws he squeezed away, teasing her.

'No games,' she insisted. 'Come here.'

Yemi continued to elude Calen. Over and over he slipped from her grasp.

Heebra nodded appreciatively. 'His flight has achieved a deftness and precision even you cannot master, Calen.'

Rachel clung to Morpeth. She could barely control her feelings. Ever since Yemi arrived she had been deliberately ignoring him. While his greeting magic bathed her like a warm stream she sent it back with cold, definite rejections. How she yearned just to hold him, but when the Witches launched their assault on her he must not be near…

'Leave him,' Heebra told Calen, when it was obvious her daughter could never again catch Yemi unless he wished it. 'Just don't antagonize the boy.' She stretched up to her full height, looking down on Rachel. 'Are you ready to defend yourself?'

Rachel did not reply, She stared at Larpskendya. And the Great Wizard stared back. He was burning for her to notice him.

'No use expecting assistance there,' gloated Heebra. 'Bound with spell-thread, he is as powerless as one of your own adults.'

Rachel looked into Larpskendya's many-coloured eyes. Inside them she saw a picture: Yemi. A movement showed Rachel what Larpskendya wanted her to do. She blinked. No. That couldn't be correct. She must have misunderstood. She narrowed her eyes, peering more closely.

'No!' Rachel yelled. 'I won't do it!'

Larpskendya's eyes overflowed with tears. But they were also hard, insistent, willing Rachel to trust him.

On Heebra's signal the Witches designated to kill Rachel opened their jaws. Death-spells streamed from their connected mouths.

Eric had time to destroy the first two, but the shock wave of the third threw him and Heiki into the air. They landed several feet away and lay in the snow, still. Moments later the stunned prapsies tumbled like stones from Eric's pockets.

Morpeth pushed Rachel down and spread his body across hers, trying to take the impact of as many blows as he could. But the death-spells merely knocked him savagely aside – and sank into Rachel.

The instant the first spell struck her Rachel wept, but not from the pain. She felt no pain. As soon as the spell touched her body she deflected its aim.

Without taking her eyes from Larpskendya she turned all the attacks of the Witches – every lethal one of them – on Yemi.

18

the butterfly child

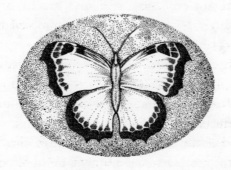

At the first touch of the death-spells Yemi's butterflies transformed.

The same dainty yellow wings that a moment earlier had been idly flapping became a hardened shield. Across his entire body they spread: he felt nothing.

Most of the Witches immediately stopped their attacks. Two did not stop. They had waited a long time for a fight, any fight, and hardly cared whether it was Yemi or Rachel they dispatched. Then one was thrown backwards. Howling, she pressed her smoking eyes into the snow. The second Witch fell to her knees, one of her lungs punctured.

'Leave him, you fools!' ordered Heebra. 'Can't you see what the boy's doing?'

Calen stared in amazement. 'He's throwing their *own spells* back at them!'

The attacks ended and everyone gazed at the space containing Yemi.

For a while he could not be seen. Steam from the snow boiled by the death-spells rose all about him. When the haze lifted everyone saw that he had no wounds. The attacks had not even dented Yemi's mood. With simple curiosity he grasped at the rising tendrils of warm air. His yellow shield had vanished, separated once again into the many and delicate butterflies. A few of these had scorched wings, nothing worse.

Most of the Witches, seeing their two injured sisters, expected Heebra to approve a renewed assault.

'Wait!' she said. 'Don't touch the baby!' No Witch was dead, she realized with relief. Only a blind Witch, humiliated, but too badly injured to launch any more attacks. 'There has been no sister killed,' Heebra called out. 'Contain yourselves. I will destroy anyone who attempts a spell against Yemi or Rachel!'

Her Witches obeyed restively, whispering in murderous tones.

'What kind of organism is he, Mother?' asked Calen, flying across. She kept her distance from Yemi. 'Is he something of Larpskendya's making? Not human, surely.'

'Human, yes.' Heebra answered. 'An exceptional evolution of magic. He must be unique – a rogue – even in this species.' She glanced warily up at Larpskendya. Even spellbound, she knew he had somehow managed to summon the boy. What else was he planning? She saw a look pass between him and Rachel.

'Cover the Wizard's eyes!' she raged at the nearest Witches. 'Bind him completely and press his face to the floor!'

Larpskendya's head was pushed below the window. Rachel shivered, not knowing what to do next – he had not had time to show her. Hearing her own laboured breathing, she realized how quiet it had become. Yemi's baby voice could be heard grumbling at Calen – an eerie noise in this place filled with so much despair. The only other sound was the rustle of dresses. It came from hundreds of Witches circling almost silently overhead, watching her.

Eric and Heiki lay stunned and scattered across the snow. The prapsies, half-senseless themselves, twitched beside Eric's neck, trying to console him with their babble. Morpeth was closer. Instinctively, Rachel made her way towards him.

Heebra saw this, but was more interested in Yemi. Calen's attempts to charm him into her arms had failed. At one point she did manage to pluck a butterfly from his nose – but Yemi snatched it back, scowling at her.

'He no longer appears to like me,' Calen said.

'He never liked you,' Heebra replied. 'It was your magic that interested him. It seems that he is no longer impressed.'

Calen peered uncertainly at the Camberwell Beauties. 'What are these strange insects, Mother?'

'Merely butterflies, nothing more,' said Heebra. 'Yemi's magic changes them into what he likes or needs.'

'But he's only a baby. How can he do this?'

'His magic is far more advanced than his human understanding,' said Heebra. 'The baby mind of Yemi senses no threat, but his magic recognizes it. I want you to take him away from here, Calen. There is a bond between Yemi and Rachel that could be dangerous, and some sisters still want to harm him. Let's remove that temptation.'

Calen nodded and reached out for Yemi. Expertly, he shifted a short distance away.

'Stop grasping at him,' Heebra told her. 'You know he craves human-type gestures. Offer him the simple affections he wants. Behave more like a mother. Caress him. Put your lips on his cheek.'

'A kiss?'

'Yes, as nearly as you can.'

It was a painful spectacle. Calen's mouths were not made for such tender gestures. As she pressed them closer to Yemi's face, the jaws reached out alarmingly – his warm smell and touch, mixed with their own juices, driving them wild.

'Get on with it,' Heebra said. 'I want to finish Rachel off.'

Yemi pushed the teeth away in disgust. Thrusting back from Calen, he started to drift hesitantly towards Rachel. He gave her his best smile, but she ignored him. Why? Confused, he continued to send out hopeful magical inquiries for her company, entreating her to be his friend.

Only by steadfastly not looking at Yemi could Rachel manage to keep up her spiky rejections. All she wanted to do was take him far, far from this dreadful place, but that was not possible.

Reaching Morpeth, she felt for his injuries. Gently, with the utmost care, she probed his back. His spinal column was severed in several places, her spells told her. I could repair the damage, she thought bitterly, but the Witches will never allow me to complete the task. Realizing this, her tears fell on Morpeth's face. As they did so he opened his bright eyes.

'We're not finished yet,' he rasped. 'I'm not finished, and neither are you. Pull me up.'

'I can't,' Rachel murmured. 'Your spine is broken.' Keeping still, trying not to attract the attention of the Witches, she used her magic to make him feel slightly more comfortable.

'Don't do that,' Morpeth said. 'I need to remain conscious. The pain helps. Tell me what happened.' She explained the way Yemi's butterflies had responded to the death-spells.

'Of course,' he said, a spasm rocking him. Furiously he fought to stay conscious, his body shaking with the effort. 'Keep up the Witch attacks on Yemi,' he urged. 'Make them continue. It's a chance.'

'I can't,' Rachel protested. 'Morpeth, don't you understand? Heebra's called her Witches off. They won't touch him now.'

Morpeth stared at the sky. The main force of the Witches stared back at him, wheeling above his head like flocks of colossal birds. Most simply kept watch over him, but a few swooped lower, shouting insults and slashing their claws above his face.

'They're impatient to continue the fight,' Morpeth said,

his voice barely audible now. 'Good. That is what we want. Come closer to me.' Rachel put her ear to his lips. Moments later, when she lifted her hair from his cheeks, he was unconscious.

Rachel did not try to wake him. She rose immediately and headed towards Eric. On the way she paused briefly by Heiki and did her best to ease her breathing – that would have to do.

Eric's body had fallen into a small hollow. He should have been covered with falling snow, but the recovering prapsies had kept the flakes off him. As Rachel approached they were busy licking his face and butting him with their plump chins, trying to nuzzle him into wakefulness.

Rachel gently nudged them aside – and used a fast-healing spell to rouse Eric.

'What's going on?' he asked, reaching straight for the prapsies to reassure himself they were safe.

'It's all right,' Rachel whispered. 'Listen, we haven't got much time...'

While Eric levered himself sorely up, Rachel tried to harden her heart to Yemi. It was the only way ...

'Are you ready?' she asked.

Eric nodded.

Nearby, Heebra watched her daughter still trying to inter-est Yemi. He would no longer let Calen close. The boy's magic has already outgrown her, Heebra realized. From now onward, she would need to train Yemi herself, using—

Suddenly, behind, she sensed a death-spell being prepared.

She turned. It was the blinded Witch. Tottering in the snow, she sniffed for Yemi, trying to identify his smell over the stench of her own burnt skin. With every moment her strength improved.

Rachel's doing, Heebra sensed at once. Rachel is healing her.

The blinded Witch opened her four mouths in a single penetrating attack.

'Stop!' Heebra cried, forming a spell to kill her own Witch.

'Now!' Rachel called.

Eric lifted his finger – and Heebra's spell evaporated. She tried to remake it – and could not. Never having faced this situation before Heebra, just for a moment, was confused.

The blinded Witch launched her spell.

It never reached Yemi. This time his butterflies were ready. One swallowed the spell. Another sent it back to the blinded Witch. She fell dead instantly.

Six blood-related sisters of the dead Witch came after him at once. None of the other Witches interfered. This was now a clear retribution kill, and they had every right to revenge the death. The sisters unsheathed their teeth and drew together, flying vertically down the sky.

Heebra hastily placed a shield around Yemi that no spells could penetrate.

Again, Eric destroyed it.

The sisters descended on Yemi. As they approached they altered formation. Splitting the pack, they came after him in twos – a classical triangular attack. The eldest sister led them, an experienced fighter, patiently withholding the decision about what death-spell to use until the last possible moment. Finally, her soul-snake named it – and the mouths of all the sisters simultaneously filled with flame.

Instantly those flames tore down their own throats. All the other Witches stared in disbelief as the entire family of sisters fell soundlessly from the air, their black dresses burning like rags in the wind.

There was silence, absolute silence. And then, from the remaining Witch packs, there came an outraged pouring forth of wrath. Heebra saw all her Witches preparing to join the fight against Yemi. With so many dead sisters now strewn across the snow, nothing could hold them back.

'Step aside,' she said to Calen, striding across. 'Yemi is too dangerous to leave alive. I will dispose of him myself.' She exuded all her magical power to attract Yemi. 'Come boy,' Heebra said, smiling. 'I know you want to.'

'No!' screamed a voice.

It was Paul. With a great cry he flew across the snow. He did not come alone. He came with Marshall and all the other children in one tremendous line of fast flight. The guarding Witches restrained a few, but most bridged the short gap to Heebra.

Paul arrived first. He threw himself at her face. Heebra swatted him aside, but she could not stop all of them. The children surged into her, driving her back from Yemi. For a few moments Heebra lay under their small hands, feeling the irritation of clawless fingers and simplistic spells.

Then, in one easy move, she threw everyone off, made a final lunge for Yemi – and breathed into his mouth.

The words went into his body.

'Oh no,' said Eric.

Yemi wailed. It was a high-pitched cry, followed by dozens more: his Camberwell Beauties. Yemi clutched at them in despair. He coughed, sagged, held his throat. Something hurt inside. He reached for Heebra's dress, not understanding that she was the cause. Heebra kicked him off and walked away.

'Why didn't you stop the spell?' Rachel railed at Eric. 'Yemi's no match for Heebra! Why didn't you stop it? Why, Eric?'

'I didn't see it,' he murmured. 'She ... she ... disguised her spell from me.'

Yemi crawled a few yards after Heebra. Then he fell on his face. At the same time his butterflies shrank back to their normal size – in his pain Yemi had forgotten them. The Camberwell Beauties had lost their magical properties. A cloud of yellow, they rose.

Abandoning him.

'No!' wailed Rachel.

Racing across the snow, she swept Yemi up, placed him in her lap and cradled his head. Gently opening his mouth, she sent her information spells into his body to discover the kind of weapon Heebra had used. And then she felt it – deep inside Yemi – an extraordinary spell of his own trying to form. She bent her face towards his, and his mouth opened wider.

Heebra saw the danger. 'Kill Rachel!' she ordered her Witches. 'The boy can do nothing without her now.'

Yemi's breath was only a murmur. Rachel pressed her

lips to his. The new spell struggled up his throat, trying to reach her, to live. She drew it out, holding it in her mouth.

'Stop her!' shrieked Heebra.

As Rachel blew the spell outwards, Heebra flew across the snow, trying to capture it. But the spell slipped through her claws. In a rippling circle, on a thrilling breeze, it flowed in all directions away from the Pole.

Rachel stared wildly at Eric. 'What kind of spell is it?'

'Some kind of awakening,' he cried. 'And I think I know what it's looking for.'

'What?'

Eric's eyes shone. 'Children, Rachel. It's looking for children!'

19

awakening

Yemi's spell left the Pole, expanding rapidly across the ice and snow.

The first children it reached lived in the Norwegian fishing town of Hammerfest, in the far north of the world. It was late here, after midnight, but the summer sun shone as it always did at this latitude on the warm sleeping children. Like a sigh the awakening spell entered the open windows. Where windows were closed it swept down a chimney. Where there was no chimney it squeezed between the smallest cracks in timber or brickwork. Nothing could stop it.

It passed across beds; a light touch – only a breath – but children awoke at once. Youngsters in dozens of homes clenched their toys. Babies rattled their cots together to the same rhythm. Older children leapt from their mattresses and ran to windows as the magic they had always possessed was released.

The spell gathered pace. There was no time to waste. Spreading in a great ring over the Arctic seas, it pushed out: across Baffin Bay into Canada, over the Kara Sea into the West Siberian Plain, down northern Finland, following the smell of children to Ivalo and beyond. And, from their rooms, in countries hundreds of miles apart, children who had never met suddenly sensed each other.

The spell moved on. It flowed with the Mackenzie river down to Fort Good Hope, Alaska. It slashed by the Canadian-American great lakes: Michigan, Ontario, Erie. But Yemi needed more. So he sent the spell into the dark portion of the northern hemisphere. In Naples, Italy, it found two boys stealing car tyres; they changed their minds. It blew across children dreaming in Tashkent and Toulouse. When their eyes opened, they glimmered silver.

The spell crossed the equator. It delved in attics, school yards, shanty huts. It followed kids playing truant in Peru and caught them. It found girls skipping in Australia and made them trip. It sought underground, into filthy sweat shops and inhuman places where child-slaves perpetually dwell. Here children dropped their tools and held hands, knowing nothing would ever be the same again.

Into deep Africa the spell travelled, to a special destination: Fiditi. There it discovered Fola, and woke her. From her mat she wept when she recognized the voice of her brother.

The spell gushed across the entire globe. It did not stop

and it did not pause or slow down until every child in the whole wide day-and-night world felt its radiant touch.

But – at the pole – Rachel knelt in the snows, with Yemi trembling in her arms.

He was barely alive now. Heebra's death-spell gripped and gripped him in its savage joy, and Rachel's own magic could only slow down its biting attack. Yemi's warm brown eyes were vacant, almost shut.

But he still commanded his awakening spell. He changed it. No more gentleness. Yemi had never intended just to awaken the magic in children. He needed their magic. It was the only way he knew to fight Heebra's death-spell.

His awakening spell became a *feeding* spell.

Only the children at the Pole were spared. Without warning, Yemi felt for the new magic of all other children – and took it. There was no time to be kind. Yemi knew only his pain, his terrible need. So he ripped away the magic of each child on Earth – left them nothing – and pulled it like a great tide towards his aching body.

A sound came then that emptied all tranquillity from the world.

It was a scream. It was the sound of all the world's children, billions of them, screaming at the same time. They could not bear this loss. For a few moments every child had known how empty their lives had been without magic; now that emptiness returned, and they would not accept it. They reacted angrily. Following their stolen magic the rage of all children streamed to the Pole.

Rachel cradled Yemi's head as the early traces of children's magic entered him. At first the magic was a trickle creeping under his lids. Then he opened his eyes wide and it poured inside, until his little body seemed about to burst with an unbearable brightness. He sighed, relaxed, breathed again. Rachel felt the magic rolling down his throat, into his lungs, his poisoned veins and near-dead heart, attacking Heebra's malice.

Healing him.

But close behind the magic came the rage. It had almost reached the Pole.

Rachel had no idea what it meant. The disarrayed Witches felt it, and looked to Heebra in bewilderment. How they looked for her leadership now!

Heebra recognized what was coming. She knew that nothing could withstand the anger Yemi had unknowingly unleashed. It was too vast. It was a pulverizing fist of anguish. No living thing at the Pole would survive this anger: not her, not Larpskendya, none of her Witches; none of the children; even Yemi would be smashed. It would obliterate everything.

There was barely time to decide what to do. Heebra stared at Yemi. How she detested this rogue child, unable even to take pleasure from the Witches he had killed. Rachel she had underestimated. I see now, she thought, how you could have fought so magnificently against Dragwena. For Larpskendya she felt only the ancient hatred. There was no time to enjoy killing him now. Somehow, even thread-bound, she had allowed him to outwit her. That hurt most of all.

Heebra wanted to observe the death agonies of her enemies, but she knew she could not even have that pleasure. She must save her High Witches. All the finest were here. If they died the majesty of Ool would die with them.

Tenderly she whispered a few words to Mak. He raised his heavy golden head, ready to protect her for the last time.

'What is it?' asked Calen, flying over. 'What's happening?'

'I have no time to explain,' said Heebra. 'Lead the sisters away, every one. Fly close in one direction, and I will keep a safe path open for as long as I can.'

Calen trembled. 'Mother, no, surely. I will not go without you. We will stand and fight together!'

'This is not a contest I can win, with or without your help,' said Heebra. 'Take my Witches from this miserable world. You are their leader now!'

'I am...not ready to rule,' Calen beseeched her. 'I can't—'

'Get away!' wailed Heebra, sounding an alarm across the sky.

Uncertainly, in small nervous bunches, her Witches rose from the snows. Calen drew them south and Heebra spread her four jaws wide. A narrow cone of green light emerged from her lips. Understanding, the Witches came together inside it. Upwards into the thick clouds they flew, continually glancing back at Heebra.

'Hurry!' roared Heebra – and then she roared again.

The rage of the children had struck the pole.

Heebra prepared herself. She had faced High Witches of the greatest intellect and imagination. She had defeated countless Doomspells. This was worse: like a thousand barbarous Doomspells. She raised Mak high, attracting the rage to her.

And the rage eagerly followed. Mak swallowed what he could. When he could take no more Heebra opened her own jaws. The rage flowed in. She held her arms wide, buckling and shuddering as the fury filled her.

The children at the Pole did not watch, or watched, if they could bear it.

Heebra contained the rage for as long as she could. Finally, with only a few of her Witches still on the Pole, she relented. The anger burst as fire from her nostrils, and then from her mouths and eyes – not little tongues of fire, but huge swollen torrents, blasting in all directions. Heebra threw her smouldering head from side to side, spewing the cleaning spiders from her jaws. Mak flopped against her neck, still desperately trying to shield her.

Heebra had time for a final bitter realization: the Griddas; she should never have released them. Only she had been able to contain their ferociousness. With her gone they would take control of Ool, and their first act would be to slay Calen, the new Witch leader. Calen would try to rally a defence, but Heebra knew her daughter was too young and inexperienced to lead the High Witches. When Calen most needed the Sisterhood they would desert her.

In her darkening mind, as her mouths closed for the last time, Heebra pictured what would happen. Calen would not hide. She would wait defiantly at the Great Tower while the Griddas gleefully climbed the walls. Calen would meet her end alone: motherless, sisterless, with only a brazen Nylo to defend her.

Heebra lay her burning head down upon the snow, and died.

20

flight

All the children gazed numbly at the smoking remains of Heebra.

The rage ended with the last vapours rising from her body, but a few scattered Witches still lay burning in the snow. No one spoke. The scene was difficult to bear, and for a long time the children simply stayed close to each other and tried to make sense of what they had witnessed.

Rachel left Yemi in Eric's care and tiptoed around the dead Witches until she found Morpeth. He lay on his back in exactly the same position she had left him, his eyes shut. Afraid that her touch might injure him further, she knelt close, asking her spells to determine the safest places to work on. With a subtlety and carefulness Rachel did not know they possessed, the major and minor spells combined to knit the bones and cauterize the internal bleeding.

Eventually Morpeth's eyes parted. 'It seems I'm not dead after all,' he murmured, managing a semi-smile.

Rachel kissed him and moved across to Heiki. Her wounds were less serious, and there was nothing wrong with her throat, but throughout the healing process Heiki said nothing. Her washed-out blue eyes were tense, not quite able to meet Rachel's.

At last, in a voice that cracked, she asked, 'Can you…' She stopped, but Rachel could read the words Heiki tried to say: forgive me.

As answer Rachel simply lifted her hand and felt Heiki's pale cheek. It was only a touch, the slightest of pressures, but Heiki reacted as if struck by a spell. She started to weep, and, seeing that, Rachel found herself also weeping. For more reasons than either could name they held each other and wept over and over, their hot tears melting tiny holes in the snow. Finally, Rachel tilted her head at the ice prison still containing Larpskendya.

'Shall we go to him together?'

'Yes!' Heiki took Rachel's hand; arm-in-arm, they flew to the Wizard. Halfway up the glistening white walls of the prison, Heiki faltered. Wincing with pain she started to slip down. Rachel caught her and carried her the remaining floors to the top.

Larpskendya lay on his side against the harsh ice. The fleeing Witches had left his arms, legs and head grotesquely tied with spell-thread. The thread was impervious to magic, so Rachel and Heiki worked with their fingers and nails only. Slowly, taking great care, they gradually loosened and removed the thick, cutting cords.

The freed Larpskendya turned at once to Rachel and Heiki. He stood shakily, towering above both girls, and drew them into his wide embrace. As they lay inside that warm space, they had never known such peace.

'Well,' Larpskendya said at last, 'we are only beginning.'

They glided to the snows below, and Rachel once again took Yemi from Eric.

Larpskendya went straight to Morpeth. He finished repairing his injuries, and then, as Morpeth struggled to his feet, Larpskendya knelt. He knelt before Morpeth, and gripped Morpeth's arm, and for a moment, when their eyes met, Morpeth saw Trimak, Fenagel and the Sarren he had left on Ithrea. All of his old friends were there, playing with magic in the glades.

'Safe and well,' Larpskendya told him quietly. 'They owe you so much, but I wonder if I owe you even more. Two worlds you have guarded now for me. How can I repay that debt?'

Morpeth shrugged self-consciously. 'There is something I miss. I—'

Larpskendya knew what he wanted. Morpeth gasped as he felt his magic seeping back. Familiar old spells trod noisily into his mind, searching for the usual places they liked to stay. Morpeth tried to thank Larpskendya, but he was too overcome to speak.

Larpskendya left him and attended to the rest of the children. They were gathered in various states of mind: disturbed, relieved, frightened, and weary, so weary from their long appalling ordeal. Most looked at the sky as if they did not really believe the Witches had departed. Larpskendya moved amongst them, reassuring each child, especially the youngest, giving them all the time they needed or wanted. He took a spiky-haired boy aside and spoke at length. Paul could not take his eyes off the Wizard.

Eric wanted to approach as well, but the prapsies kept shoving their heads out of his coat and poking tongues at Larpskendya.

'Stop it, boys,' Eric warned them. 'Don't you recognize who that is?'

They turned around and wiggled their feathery backsides at the Wizard. He looked up, catching them at it.

The prapsies gulped, hiding behind their wings as Larpskendya strode across.

'That won't do any good,' Eric said. 'You're both for it now. Me too, probably. Start bowing fast.'

Both prapsies bowed at Eric.

'Not at *me*,' he sighed. 'Flipping heck…'

He tried to twist them to face the approaching Larpskendya, but the Wizard had already bridged the gap. He picked both prapsies up and swung them close to his face. One stuck out a tongue, tasting his ear. 'Ugh!' it said. Larpskendya laughed and placed both prapsies on Eric's shoulders. And then Larpskendya bent towards Eric, and they shared words Eric would never forget or tell.

Finally Larpskendya brought Yemi, Rachel, Heiki, Eric and Morpeth together. Rachel spread Yemi on her lap. He was a thing of astonishing beauty. Unendurably vibrant colours teemed in his eyes, spilling from the edges, too much for him to bear. Yet he still tried to cover them with his small hands, as if not wishing to let them go.

'All the magic of the world's children is inside him,' Larpskendya said. 'Our little thief does not want to give it back. We must help him.'

'Let me,' said Rachel.

She knelt alongside Yemi, prising the fingers from his eyelids. She kissed him.

With a tiny cry he suddenly wept.

He threw his arms around Rachel's neck – and his eyes opened. Spells instantly burst out, not one spell but dozens, then thousands, all wanting to be first. They emerged in every imaginable colour and left the pole, heading determinedly back to their original owners. In a few minutes the transformation was complete. Morpeth listened closely – and heard a sound.

It was a sound of surprise – a blissful intake of breath from all children.

With the release of the magic Yemi became himself again, and his Camberwell Beauties returned. They covered Rachel's body, their skinny black legs trying to draw her closer to him. Paul and Marshall came warily over, along with the other children, and the butterflies fluttered on them all, one or two landing on each child.

'Home,' Rachel beseeched Larpskendya. 'Can we take him home? Can we?'

Immediately Larpskendya shifted them, so smoothly that none of the children felt a thing.

It was dark; night-time in Fiditi. They stood outside Yemi's house, and normally at this hour it would have been quiet. But the entire village bustled with life. All the children were awake – and busy. One young girl skimmed like a dragonfly over the river Odooba. Her silver eyes lit the surface, attracting mosquitoes. From the dense rainforest nearby came the noise of a group of screeching Colobus monkeys. Two boys had woken them. Perched alongside in the frailest upper branches of a tree, they laughed and screeched back. Eric saw a toddler trying to fly over a leafy bush. He didn't quite make it, and ruefully rubbed his scraped legs. Two teenage girls kneeled face to face outside a hut, changing the shape of each other's hair. A scruffy-looking boy sat at a window, idly blowing clouds back and forth across the sky.

Morpeth gazed at Rachel wistfully. 'Can you believe all this? And things like it must be happening everywhere tonight across the world. Everywhere!'

'I know.' She thought about the little French boy, so recently crying for his lovely melting rainbow. Was he running back up to his mountains now? Or perhaps he had already learned how to fly ...

A bird shot past Morpeth, landing like the tamest of falcons on a thin boy's wrist. A girl lay dreamily on her back, watching a tuft of grass rise from the ground and tickle her brother's neck.

'I wish,' Eric said to Paul, 'that I could be everywhere at once tonight. To see it all.'

'Don't you feel jealous?' Paul asked. 'I mean, you're the only kid in the world left without magic.'

'No one else can do what I can,' Eric said simply.

Both prapsies nodded so hard their heads nearly snapped off.

The front door of Yemi's house opened – just a crack. Inside there were whispers. Finally Fola came out. Her eyes gleamed silver, like the others, and when she saw Larpskendya she curtsied over and over, not quite sure how to behave.

'It's all right,' Rachel reassured her. 'Join us. What's wrong?'

Fola lingered at the door, obviously waiting for something. Then, almost creeping forth, Yemi's mother emerged. She looked horrified by what had happened, afraid even to look at any of the village children – as if their eyes might burn. Yemi threw himself on her. She shrank back. When Yemi insisted, following her, his mother reluctantly let him settle against her chest. At his touch she relaxed slightly, but still stroked his head as though it was a breakable and slightly strange object.

Fola shrugged at Rachel. 'Mama not ready yet. We must be gentle to her, and them all.' She indicated a few adults nearby.

Until now Rachel had not noticed the rest of the adults. Compared with the animated, eyes-glowing children they were like shadows, mainly staying in the background. All appeared hopelessly bemused, some uncertain about approaching their own children. One father crouched under his hovering daughter, obviously expecting her to simply fall from the sky. A few parents stayed indoors, too afraid even to come out.

Rachel thought of Mum, and suddenly wanted her close. And then she thought of Dad, and felt anxious. She spoke to Larpskendya – and they shifted again to Rachel's home.

Mum and Dad were standing in the front porch, looking outward. Seeing Rachel and Eric, their faces broke with relief. Rachel looked happily at her dad. He was well, and tearful, and almost crushed her with one arm, while doing the same to Eric with the other. Then, seeing Larpskendya, Dad broke off for a moment and, almost formally, shook his hand.

Finally everyone turned to look at the world beyond the porch. There was so much to see. Overhead, girls danced on a slanting roof. Higher up a group of kids Eric recognized spiralled like midges around a block of council flats, their laughter carrying for miles in the mild summer air. Boys played cricket in the clouds. Other children were off alone, accompanying planes, following birds, or a hundred other things they had woken in the night. A boy in a wheelchair chased down a greyhound. One small girl simply read a book by the light of her own incandescent eyes. And all around, wherever the children stood or ran or flew, they left their telltale individual trails: smells new to the Earth – the scents of magic.

'I knew you would be safe,' Mum whispered to her children, watching it all. 'As soon as I saw all this happening—' she flapped her arms around – 'I *knew*.' She turned to Larpskendya. 'There's no changing things back the way they were, is there?'

Larpskendya shook his head.

Morpeth marvelled at the activity all around. 'Look at the magic they're performing!' he cried. 'On Ithrea we saw some amazing things, at the end, but those people had practised for centuries. How has it taken these children such a short time to learn similar skills?'

'No world has ever been held back as long as yours,' Larpskendya explained. 'Or had its magic released so quickly.' His voice became filled with humility. 'I have no idea what else might happen tonight. There has never been such a flowering! This' – he indicated the sky, grass, moon, and children who moved so gracefully between them – 'is your future, the beginning of an indescribable adventure for all children. Soon making magic will come as easily to you as breathing.' He smiled. 'And then, of course, it will no longer seem like magic at all.'

Everyone looked down the street, where a scared dad hollered at the sky. His young son was diving recklessly through narrow alleyways, far too excited to notice.

Rachel sidled up to Morpeth. 'This new world's going to be dangerous for the adults, isn't it? Everything will be different for them as well.'

Morpeth nodded. 'Most will be envious of their children. And kids won't automatically do what they're told any longer, either. If parents try to make them … well …'

'Anything might happen,' whispered Rachel, shuffling closer to Mum and Dad. A chilling image jumped at her: of kids taking control, and parents, not safe to go out alone, having to be escorted and cared for by their own children.

Heiki stood next to Larpskendya, watching a girl copying a leaf falling through the air.

'When this all settles down,' she inquired, 'won't the kids form into packs? Magic gangs, selected by skill, with the toughest in charge? That's what the Witches planned.'

'Yes,' said Larpskendya. 'That will happen in some places.' He stared at her. 'Everything you can imagine may happen now.'

'Can't you tell how our magic is going to develop?' Rachel asked him. 'Don't *you* know?'

'Magic evolves differently on all worlds,' he told her. 'But Earth is uniquely bountiful. There has never been a race as gifted as yours, so early in its history.'

'Is that why the Witches are interested in us?' Heiki wondered.

'Yes. They want you so much. And you are not a secret from them any longer.'

Morpeth shivered. 'For how long are we safe?'

'I cannot answer that,' Larpskendya said. 'But the Witches will never leave you in peace now. They will regroup and return in larger numbers. The endless war against us is all they know, and they have seen how useful you can be. Yemi, especially, will tantalize them. Who knows what he will be capable of soon?'

Rachel gently touched the deep claw marks still on Larpskendya's neck, but they did not heal.

'Leave them,' Larpskendya said. 'As a reminder of what I have unleashed.' He turned sadly to address Morpeth, Eric and Rachel, Mum and Dad. 'There is a new enemy now: the Griddas are loose. I knew Heebra was becoming desperate, but I never thought she would release their fury.' He hung his head. 'I pushed her too far, too quickly, these last years. That was a terrible mistake.'

Over Rachel's house two shining goal posts appeared. Moonlit figures passed the football perfectly.

'They don't fear the arrival of the Griddas yet,' Morpeth said gratefully. Whatever the future held, tonight his heart felt light, and he could barely follow all the children teeming amongst the night clouds. He wanted to join them.

'That is true,' Larpskendya said solemnly. 'Why should they fear?' And then, suddenly, in a deliberate, measured way he assessed all those children pressed so closely to him. Finally he gazed at Rachel, as if he saw in her a summary of all their worth. Her eyes, staring into his, were the colour of gladness.

Larpskendya's expression became almost desperately, achingly hopeful.

'I want to show you something,' he said. 'You need to understand the great challenge ahead.'

'Show us what?' asked Dad suspiciously.

'Another world. A precious world. For many lifetimes the Witches have wanted to crush its loveliness.'

Eric blinked uncertainly. 'Is it far?'

'Far and near. Nowhere is too remote for you now. We can fly there.'

'What? Tonight?'

Larpskendya smiled. 'Why not?'

'What about the prapsies? I'm not going without them …'

Larpskendya swept his arms, taking in the scope of the sky. 'We'll take everyone.'

The prapsies chuckled haltingly, not sure what he meant.

'What do you mean, everyone?' Dad asked. 'You mean all the youngsters here?' He indicated the nearest children. 'All *these*?'

Larpskendya's eyes shone. 'No, you don't understand. I mean *everyone*. I mean every child and adult on your world. All of them.'

'Yes!' Rachel cried. 'Yes!'

Larpskendya breathed in and suddenly Rachel felt a tightening inside her, as if millions of minds were being drawn together. When she looked up she saw children all around lifting their chins to the same constellation of stars in the western sky.

Eric glanced at Mum and Dad, thinking they wouldn't enjoy this one bit. But he was wrong.

'Like this?' Mum stretched her arms out timidly. 'Well, am I doing it right?'

Larpskendya laughed, a long and booming laugh that shook off any final fears he may have had. 'Yes, that will do well enough,' he said. He paused and gazed at Rachel, Morpeth and Eric. 'Are you ready?'

They nodded tightly.

'Blimey, boys,' muttered one of the prapsies. 'What's going on?'

But there was no time for its companion to answer. From homes, from ships, from jets at thirty thousand feet and mines deeper still, and from the child-filled skies, everyone in the world raised their eyes.

And, a moment later, only animals and plants breathed on this Earth.

a chapter from

the wizard's promise

Book Three of *The Doomspell* sequence

1

schools without children

As Rachel awoke, her information spells automatically swept the house for threats. They probed into each room, an extra set of senses watching out for her.

Nothing out of the ordinary, they reported. Mum lay in her usual morning bath. Dad was in the study, trying to touch his toes. The information spells delved further out. In the garden, two froglets were wondering whether to make a break for it across the dangerous lawn. Next door's dog hid behind a shed, thinking no one else knew about his juicy bone.

Rachel smiled, peering out of her bedroom window. A flock of geese passed by, and, just for a moment, as she gazed up at those birds, and listened to the familiar sounds of home and garden, it was as if nothing had changed in the world.

Then a group of under-fives cut across the sky.

The youngsters flew in tight formation, led by a boy. Rachel guessed he might be three years old, probably less. The group travelled with arms pinned neatly to their sides, little heads thrust proudly ahead. Their eyes all shone some tint of blue, the distinctive colour of flying spells.

The slower geese scattered nervously when the children crossed their path.

Getting up, Rachel brushed out her long dark hair and strolled downstairs to the kitchen. Her younger brother, Eric, sat at the dining table. A bowl of cornflakes crackled satisfyingly in front of him.

'You know, if I had magic,' he said, tucking in, 'I wouldn't bother with flying or the other stuff. I'd just use a spell to keep the taste of cornflakes in my mouth forever.'

'You'd soon get sick of it,' Rachel answered.

'No,' Eric said earnestly. 'I wouldn't.' He waved his spoon at the departing toddlers. 'Those little 'uns are probably long-distance racers. Must be, practising like that. They're so *serious*. At their age I was still happy just chucking things at you.'

'Mm.' Rachel glanced round, expecting to see the prapsies. The prapsies were a mischievous pair of creatures – feathered body of a crow, topped with a baby's face – that had once served a Witch on another world. Usually Eric put them up to some prank when Rachel first came down in the morning.

'Where are the boys then?' she asked warily.

'I let them out early for a change,' Eric said. 'Told them to find me a gift, something interesting.'

'Did you send them far?'

'China.'

'Good.'

Rachel stared up at the rooftops of the town. It was a typical morning, with children all over the sky. A few were up high and alone, practising dead-stops in the tricky April winds. Most children had simply gathered in their usual groups in the clouds, friends laughing and joking together. A few houses down Rachel saw a boy cooing. As he did so a dove, tempted from some thicket, rose to his hand. Further away a girl drifted casually across the sky, plucking cats from gardens. The cats trailed in a long line behind her, complaining mightily.

'Hey look!' Eric cried. 'Lightning-finders!'

Six teenagers were heading purposefully south, their arms raised like spikes.

'It's a brand new game started up by the thrill-seekers,' Eric said. 'You search for heavy weather, find the storms and dodge the lightning forks. Most competitions are held in the Tropics, where the really big storms are. I bet that's where those kids are off to.' He gazed wistfully after the teenagers, who had already disappeared over the horizon.

'What happens if they get hit by the lightning?'

'Bad things, I suppose,' Eric said. 'It's risky, but that's the whole point. Wouldn't be exciting otherwise, would it?'

Rachel shrugged. The new magical games didn't interest her much. She was more interested in those children stationed in the air, watching the skies for Witches.

Nearly a year had passed since the baby boy, Yemi, had released the magic of all the children on Earth. In that first glorious Awakening, there had been a superabundance of magic – enough for the Wizard leader, Larpskendya, to transport every child and adult on Earth to Trin.

When Rachel thought of that purple-skied, plant-filled world, it still hurt. The plants of Trin had a language of leaves so rich that even the Wizards could only guess the meaning of their graceful movements. But the plants were dying. The Witches had poisoned them. On a whim, they had contaminated Trin's soils. And slowly, as their magic drained away, the Trin plants were losing their minds. Each year the great leaves waved ever more frantically in the breezes as they struggled to hear each other.

It was not possible to stay on Trin for long. The special blossoming of magic following the Awakening soon faded, and the adults and children had to return home. But everyone understood: if the Witches could do this amount of damage to Trin, a world that meant nothing to them, what would happen if they returned to Earth? So everyone had prepared. For months children practised their defensive spells. Night and day they patrolled the skies, anticipating a massed attack of Witches that never came.

Meanwhile, Ool – the Witch homeworld – wrapped itself in hush. A battle, the Wizards knew, was taking place: a battle for control, between the High Witches Rachel and other children had fought before, and the more ferocious warrior-breed, the terrifying Griddas. For a long time Ool had been silent.

Larpskendya had no doubt the Griddas had won. It worried him because the Wizards knew so little about them. The Griddas had been bred by the High Witches, bred to be savage warriors, and kept underground. But the former High Witch leader, Heebra, had made the mistake of releasing them.

And, having tasted freedom, the Griddas had turned on their makers.

As Rachel gazed up at the sky, her slim freckled face perched on her hands, she wondered how ready the people of Earth were to face the Griddas. She also missed a friend.

'I wonder,' she said, half to herself, 'how Morpeth's doing? I miss him.'

'He's only been gone a few days,' Eric protested.

'I *still* miss him.'

'Actually, so do I, but it's his only visit back to Ithrea in ages. Larpskendya's picking him up in a few weeks.'

While Rachel thought fondly about Morpeth, three girls landed beside the garden pond. They walked across the lawn, waving hopefully through the glass doors of the patio.

'Oh no, part of your fan club,' groaned Eric. 'Do they never leave off?'

A few children always loitered near the house, curious to get a glimpse of Rachel. Her reputation drew them, and the sheer quality of her magic. Every child on Earth wanted to be closer to it.

'I've seen those three before,' Eric muttered. 'Two nights ago. It was raining, pouring down, but did they care? Barmy nutters.' He pulled a face, attempting to scare the girls away. 'Clear off!' he yelled. The girls smiled sweetly back. 'They never flipping listen to me,' Eric said. 'Why don't you give them a shock, Rach? You know, send them to the Arctic or something. It'll take them at least an hour to fly back.'

Two of the girls nudged each other forward, trying to get Rachel's attention. The other one looked steadily at Eric.

A little ruffled, he self-consciously smoothed out his baggy pyjamas.

Rachel laughed. 'I'm not the only one with admirers.'

'Can't you get rid of them?'

'Oh, I think we should let that pretty-looking girl in,' Rachel said. 'I can tell she wants to talk to you.'

'Don't you dare!'

The girls stood outside, hoping for a conversation. Rachel, however, had entertained too many admirers lately. She turned away from their stares, feeling a desire to get out of the house.

'Come on,' she said. 'We'll go for a walk.'

'You're joking, aren't you?' Eric said. 'There's no chance of slipping out quietly. The sky's thick with kids.'

'I'll shift us, then.'

'Where to?'

'Let's find the prapsies. Creep up on them, give 'em a scare.'

'Hey, nice idea. Just let me get dressed.'

'*I* could dress you.'

'No way,' Eric snorted. 'I'm not having your spells fiddling with my pyjamas.'

He thumped up the stairs, colliding with Mum.

'Careful,' Mum groaned. Pinning back her wet hair, she smiled at Rachel. 'Going out, love?'

'Yep.'

'You'll need a disguise from the fans, then.' She inspected her daughter critically. 'How about an older look? Add three years on and lose the freckles. Blonde and fifteen?'

Rachel smirked. 'Blonde's out, Mum. Hair fashion's changing.'

'What's in vogue these days?'

'Silver for boys, long and slicked back. With the girls, anything crazy.'

Mum shrugged. Children regularly used magic to alter

their appearance now. Nothing surprised her any more.

'You want to come along with us, mum? I'll take you wherever you like.'

'No, you go off and enjoy yourselves. I'll potter about here.'

Eric reappeared, wearing jeans and his woolly parka coat.

'Ready?' Rachel asked.

'I was born ready.' Hoiking up his collar, Eric noticed her new round-cheeked face. 'Good disguise,' he said. 'You look dumb. That's realistic. Better hide your magic scent, too.'

Rachel did so, kissed Mum lightly on the cheek – and *shifted*.

Immediately, without any sensation of flight, she and Eric had travelled a few miles from the house. Rachel was one of the few children in the world who possessed this skill – the ability to move instantaneously from one place to another.

They stood on the outskirts of town. Above them a boy flew by on some errand or other, his dad perched on his back. Rachel heard their laughter. Magic did not survive the passage to adulthood, but adults who wanted to fly could still enjoy that special thrill through children.

Rachel and Eric tramped up a long path. It brought them to Rachel's old nursery school.

'Oh, it's closed,' Eric said. 'I hadn't heard.'

A thick chain on the school gate barred the way inside. No notice of explanation was provided, or needed.

'Same everywhere,' Rachel said. 'This was the last one. Closed last week. You know what little kids are like – just want to be out playing.' She smiled. At first it had seemed an ominous development when children stopped turning up for school. But if you could fly, why sit in a classroom? The best teachers soon realized that traditional schooling offered nothing that could rival the fascination of magic. Why bother with textbook geography, with the world at your disposal? Children now went all over the world for their education, and teachers not afraid of flying in the arms of their students went with them.

'It's funny,' Eric noted, as they walked away from the nursery. 'A couple of kids from my old school took the Head of Maths out flying yesterday. Did I tell you? Wanted to know about vectors and something called thrust quotations. Reckoned it might help them manoeuvre better in high winds.'

'Was he able to help them?'

'Yeah. They were practising with him last night,' Eric said.

'What? They took him out in the dark?'

'Sure. Why not. He was game for it, apparently. A true test for his theories, and all that. They say he enjoyed it, but it was a while before he could talk normally afterwards.'

A couple of sprinters swerved around Rachel. They flew close to the ground, the wind from their passage messing her hair. Eric laughed – knowing they were deliberately trying to goad Rachel into following them.

Flying games were the most popular new sports – fiercely competitive, fast and visible, with rules that were usually easy to master. Rachel could have won them all, and local teams were always trying to get her attention, but such displays didn't interest her. She led Eric from the nursery lane into an adjoining field. There were some rusty swings here and a dilapidated rocking horse. It was the sort of desultory old-style playground only a few children still used.

'Feebles,' Eric said, seeing two children there.

'Don't call them that,' Rachel snapped angrily. 'I *hate* that word.'

'It's what they're being called, Rach, whether you like it or not.'

A young boy and girl, seven or eight years old, sat on the wooden horse. The boy wore shorts and a wind-cheater, and looked cold. The girl had a long white skirt. She had hitched it up over her knees to help her clamber onto the frame. They sat astride the horse, rocking each other back and forth as best they could.

Eric sighed, glancing at Rachel. 'You're going to play with them, aren't you?'

'Just for a bit.'

'That's what you always say. Then it becomes hours.'

Rachel grinned. 'I like being with them. Anyway, these are new. I'm going to introduce myself. And don't call them feebles.'

The children on the rocking horse were the least talented children. Spell-gifts were not evenly distributed. After the initial rush of magic following the Awakening, it was discovered that a few children in each country had little magic – so little that it went virtually unnoticed. In a world where many children could fly effortlessly, others could still only dream of flying. None of these children could take part in the spell-games sprouting up all around, so Rachel had instead set up a programme where the most magical children spent time with them.

In the clouds above a boy the same age as the little girl sped by, way out of her reach. She longingly followed him until he passed over some hills.

'Hey, who are you two?' Rachel asked, rushing over and putting the brother and sister at ease. The girl lifted her arms, wanting to be picked up. The boy hung back shyly.

'Get on,' Rachel said to them both, lowering her back so they could climb aboard. Then, gently, she rose skyward.

'I'm not scared,' the boy said fiercely.

Rachel laughed. 'I can see that!'

"Up! Up!' the little girl told her. 'Go faster!' As Rachel increased velocity, the girl cried out, 'I'm falling. I'm falling off!'

'No, you're not,' Rachel whispered into her ear. 'I'll never let you fall off!'

The girl gripped her neck, so happy to be paid attention by a child with magic.

For a while Rachel took directions from the brother and sister about what to do. They wanted to transform, so Rachel shifted halfway across the world. Soon the little girl and her brother were disguised in Asia, creeping in tangled forests, sneaking up on tiger cubs.

Finally, after Rachel had exhausted them with many kinds of magic, she took them back home. 'I'll come here tomorrow, if you like,' she said.

The girl sucked her thumb. 'Will you?'

'Promise.' Rachel fixed a time.

She left them with a wave and shifted back to the nursery, where she found Eric scowling. 'Hey, what's going on?'

he said. 'I'm stuck out here, left like a twit by the kiddy swings. You said we were going to find the prapsies!'

'We are, we are. Stop moaning and climb on.' As Eric scrambled onto her back some of Rachel's favourite spells, her shifters, eased forward into her mind. She felt her whole body supercharging with exhilaration as they loosened up all their tremendous power.

Eric saw her eyes light up: a thousand glistening shades of blue.

'Get ready,' she told him, balancing on her toes.

'Oh-oh,' Eric said. 'A big trip, then. Where are you dragging us off to?'

'Wouldn't be a surprise if I gave it away.'

'How far? Come on. Just tell me.'

'Everest!'

'Oh no, not the flipping Himalayas again!' He seized her collar.

'Are you ready or not?'

'Yeah, yeah, I suppose.' Eric took a deep breath and half-shut his eyes. 'But you'd better keep me warm. I'm warning you, Rach. Last time we went there you nearly froze off my –'

Rachel launched into the chilly sky.